Close To You

a collection of short stories

by

Julie McGowan

SUNPENNY BOOKS
Sunpenny Publishing Group

CLOSE TO YOU

ISBN # 978-1-909278-72-1

First published in Great Britain in 2015 by Sunpenny Publishing
www.sunpenny.com (Sunpenny Publishing Group)

MORE BOOKS BY JULIE McGOWAN
Don't Pass Me By
The Mountains Between
Just One More Summer

MORE BOOKS FROM THE SUNPENNY PUBLISHING GROUP:

Blue Freedom, by Sandra Peut
Brandy Butter on Christmas Canal, by Shae O'Brien
Dance of Eagles, by JS Holloway
Embracing Change, by Debbie Roome
Far Out, by Corinna Weyreter
Going Astray, by Christine Moore
If Horses Were Wishes, by Elizabeth Sellers
Moving On, by Jenny Piper
My Sea is Wide, by Rowland Evans
Someday, Maybe, by Jenny Piper
Sophie's Quest, by Sonja Anderson
The Lost Crown of Apollo, by Suzanne Cordatos

Dedication

For Pete, my husband and best friend,
who has supported and encouraged me
since the first story was written.

Thanks

A huge thank you is due to
my family and friends, as always,
for their love and encouragement.
Also to Jo and Sunpenny Publishing
for yet another great editing and
production job. And to the readers
who buy my books, and to those who
write to magazines or to me to say
they've enjoyed my stories –
every letter and email makes my day!

Close To You is an anthology of some of the short stories Julie McGowan has had published over the years, in various magazines and other media, some of which have won awards in competitions. We at Sunpenny Publishing are proud to have released Julie's first three novels, *The Mountains Between, Just One More Summer,* and *Don't Pass Me By* – excerpts of which you will find at the end of this book, following Julie's author page. We hope you enjoy Julie's writing as much as hundreds of thousands of others have, evidenced by the fan mail she receives! *Just One More Summer* will also be released in German in December 2015, by Random House's imprint in Germany.

Contents

Rights 1

The Lustre Jug 9

Just Like James 21

Lost and Found 31

The Sofa 39

The Postcard 49

Hearing Loss 57

Worried About Jim 65

Voice of Romance 75

Close To You 89

Faint Hearts 95

Maybe 103

Miss MacGregor 109

If Dreams Were Wishes 117

Somebody to Love 125

A Pair of Blue Eyes 131

The Red Shed 139

If 147

Hay Fever 151

The Sandwich Filler 161

Red Shoes 167

Today's The Day 177

About the Author 182

The Mountains Between: Sample First Chapter 187

Just One More Summer: Sample Chapters 201

Don't Pass Me By: Sample Chapters 219

Rights

The postman's left the gate open again. I've already phoned once.

"Don't you train your staff to respect people's property?" I asked, when they eventually deigned to answer the phone. Some young girl it was on the other end. She said she'd pass my request onto their customer services manager. "It wasn't a request," I told her, "it's my right to have my property respected. The gate's there to be closed. What if children or pets got out into the road?"

"Have you got any children or pets?" she asked. Cheeky little madam.

"No I haven't," I said, "but that's not the point, is it?"

There's only one letter, anyway. From the medical panel. *Dear Mrs. Hewson, Regarding your recent medical review... we would like to see you again...*

See me again? There were three of them last time. How many doctors does it take to realise that I'm unfit to work? All the evidence was there. Took me ages to fill in that blooming form and make sure I'd remembered everything.

"Mrs. Hewson," the first one said, all oily and patronising, "it's been a year since we assessed your claim for invalidity benefit. We just want to *clarify* a few points. Tell me a bit more about the 'near fatal car crash' which you say *exacerbated* your precarious emotional state."

1

He emphasised all the long words in case I didn't understand them, or to show how clever he was. So I told him. "The *outward manifestations,*" I said, playing him at his own game, "might only have been bruising to the chest, but the *repercussions* have been dreadful. *Post traumatic stress,*" I told him. "Panic attacks. After all, I could have been killed if I'd been travelling any faster – no brake fluid apparently – it doesn't bear thinking about."

"And the 'recent death of a close and dearly-loved friend'," the next one said, pretending to be all chummy, but I know their game. They're only there to save the government money. But I know my rights. I've paid in all my life – well, until I started being unwell of course – so I'm entitled.

"You say this bereavement has caused you mental anxiety and depression," he said. "How has that been?"

So I said to this one, "Six years," I said. "Six years since I'd seen her and then I'm told she's dead with cancer. Imagine! We were the same age; it could've been me. Plays on your mind, that sort of thing."

Then the third one started. "What about your physical problems?" he said. "Difficulty with walking – you state you're in severe pain after eight hundred yards. Refresh my memory," he said, "as to the cause."

"It was when I broke my leg," I told him. "Because a bit of carpet worked loose on the stairs. I knew it hadn't mended properly – my leg, that is; my husband fixed the carpet straight away – but two years it took me before one of the doctors would agree with me, and that was only after I went private. Goes right up into my back, the pain does."

Keep it moving, keep active, I was told, so I took up line dancing. They were a bit surprised when I told them that.

"Oh yes," I said, "Three times a week I go now. Agony, of course, but I persevere. You know what they say, 'No pain, no gain'. A martyr to it, I am."

Anyway, this third doctor, he was a bit better than

the other two. "Oh, Mrs. Hewson," he says, "I do hope you've been able to park near the building."

"Ah," I said, "I was going to bring that up. Way over the other side of the grounds I had to park, and then walk up that long drive – it isn't right. Of course, if I qualified for a disabled badge..." Well, he seemed to understand, because when it was all over he actually walked me all the way back to my car. Solicitous, that's what he was, asking if I was all right when I got into the driving seat, after walking such a way. That's how a doctor should be.

Next door's started up now. Screaming at the kids again. Got no idea how to bring children up properly. I called the social workers out once – in confidence of course, because I wouldn't want her next door to feel embarrassed if she knew it was me. They didn't do anything, though. She's still at those kids all day – terrible racket she makes, shatters my nerves and sets my psoriasis off again. So I deal with it my own way. Take the portable telly through to the dining room and leave it on full blast – motor racing's the best – so she knows what it's like having that sort of noise through the party wall. I took the CD player in one morning and put Pavarotti on, top volume, and went out shopping. She went away for a few days after that, took the kids with her. Ashamed, I expect.

They're not so bad the other side, keep themselves to themselves – except for when we had the parking problem. Quite hysterical she got when I said they couldn't park their van outside our property. I told her it was blocking our light and it looked such a mess. And where were visitors to our house supposed to park?

"There's no law that says you own the kerb," she shouted at me.

"I don't know what it's like where you come from, but I know my rights," I told her, "and if you want me to take legal action I will."

I wanted Jack to go round and demand an apology

from her, but by the time he got home he said it was too late.

There's a new woman moved in over the back. I've not spoken, but Jack knows all about her. Well, he would, the way she pesters him. Always popping her head over the fence whenever he's in the garden. She's a widow, so she goes all helpless when there's a man about. All coy faces and fluttering eyes. Always telling Jack how hard it is being on her own. Hoping he's a soft touch.

Dora, her name is. Retired schoolteacher who does a couple of mornings at the charity shop. I see her sometimes when I'm looking out the front waiting for Jack to get back from his walk. She goes jogging past in a terrible pink tracksuit. I don't know what she thinks she looks like, a woman her age. I said to Jack, "She may have been a schoolmistress, but she's got no dress sense. Talk about mutton. Probably gets her own clothes from that charity shop."

Jack got back just before lunch from his daily constitutional. He's got very keen on walking since he retired. He goes out in all weathers. I've offered to go with him, for company, but he said I shouldn't on any account, not with my leg and back. He's very considerate, is Jack. Doesn't say a lot, but he's a thinker, oh yes. Goes very deep, he does. I told him what an awful morning I've had, what with the postman and the noise from next door.

"We'll have to move," I said. "This used to be a nice street, when we first came here, but no-one even speaks any more. Cross the road rather than talk to you. Too busy thinking about number one, all of them. I don't think I can stand it much longer," I said.

"No," he said, "I don't think I can, either."

He was out in the garden all afternoon. Loves his garden, Jack does. If he's not out walking, he's messing about with his borders, or in his potting shed. I don't go in the garden much, especially not if that Dora over the back's out there. It'll be different when those trees Jack planted for me have grown a bit. Give us more privacy from prying eyes.

She came out, just like I knew she would when she saw Jack. I was watching through the kitchen window, waiting for her to take advantage. She thinks she can get round him. But he didn't stand any of her nonsense. I could see him talking to her, in his measured way and nodding towards the house. Telling her. She nodded too, still working her way into his good books.

He came in a bit later, with a lovely few leeks, turned the telly off in the dining room and just said, "We don't need that any more."

See what I mean? Few words, but purposeful.

"It's not right," I told him, going back to the postman, as he started chopping up the leeks, "we shouldn't have to put up with this. It makes my migraines worse. Day in day out, on and on. It's not right at my time of life. We'll have to move. I'll tell those doctors next time just what this place is doing to my nerves – perhaps they'll put in a good word for us, write a letter or something..."

*H*e didn't mean it, I know he didn't. I told the ambulance men it was an accident – "It's all right, it's all right," I kept saying. Well, gasped more like, because it had taken my breath away a bit.

My fault really – I was so busy explaining to Jack why we needed to move, that I got in his way when he turned round and the knife just went into my stomach. Well they could see how upset he was – they could see that it wasn't his fault. White as a sheet he was with all the blood around, and shaking like a leaf. He was shaking so much he couldn't even let go of the knife – they had to take it off him. As for me, I was too surprised to scream or anything – although her next door had started up again, which more than made up for it. I didn't even feel it at first, see. Jack's always kept his knives really sharp

– so it just sort of slid in.

It was lucky that Dora turned up when she did. Came round the back with a cake for us. A cheek, really. Did she think I can't rustle up a Victoria sponge myself? But like I said, just as well she was there. Thought she was going to pass out at first. "Jack, Jack," she was saying. "It'll be all right. We'll sort everything out, you'll see. Give me the knife, my lovey... come on... let me have it." But he wouldn't – he wasn't one of her little children after all. Though he sounded a bit like one. "I can't... I can't..." he was whimpering.

"Can you help... all this blood..." I gasped. Brought her wits back, that did. "Yes... yes... of course," she said, coming over to me but keeping one eye on Jack, because he still had the knife in his hand. "I'll put this tea towel there – it looks quite clean..."

"Of course it's clean," I hissed, "Now go and call an ambulance – phone's in the hall..."

She sat with Jack while the ambulance men saw to me. But he still wouldn't give her the knife. I tried to tell her he was in shock, but I couldn't talk much by then. And poor Jack, he wasn't saying anything at all. He's still feeling so bad about it he hasn't been able to come and see me yet, even though it's been five days.

They've been pretty good at the hospital – well, once I'd got that cleaning supervisor sorted out. Filthy it was, around my bed. So I told the nurses that I wanted to speak to the cleaner. Oh no, they told me, I had to complain to the senior nurse on duty and she would speak to the 'hotel services manager', who would review my complaint and speak to the cleaner if it was appropriate. 'Hotel services manager'? In a hospital? Can you believe it? It's as bad as the Post Office. I made them fetch her to me. I told her, "If this really was a hotel," I said, "I would be asking for my money back by now – I know my rights."

They moved me to another bed, then, in the corner by the window. Their way of apologising I suppose. It's quite nice, though, with being on the ground floor. I can see people coming and going.

One of the nurses has just been and pulled the curtains round my bed. "Your husband's here to see you," she said. "We're letting him come in, even though it's not visiting time yet, because he says he has something important to talk about."

Well, I knew he was here. I saw him through the window, walking up the path. He's got that Dora woman with him – needed a bit of Dutch courage I expect. She's got her caring face on and she was patting his arm as they walked along, and talking to him. I'd rather not put up with her, of course, but perhaps she'll have the sense to wait outside.

No. Here they come together. She's still got hold of his arm. Poor man, he's looking ever so serious. I'll have to tell him that it's all right, I'm not blaming him or anything. It was an accident. He knows I've always been accident prone.

I'll tell him that I'll be home in a couple of days. That'll cheer him up.

The Lustre Jug

"Thank you, Mrs. Etheridge, I'll have the chair delivered to you first thing tomorrow."

With a sigh of relief Alexander ushered Mrs. Etheridge through the cool of the shop and out onto the sun-baked pavement. She had spent a full hour deciding whether the button-back nursing chair was the exact shade of puce to match her bedroom curtains, which she had described at great length so that Alexander would know exactly what she meant.

It was as he was closing the door that he saw her. It was only a glimpse at first as she threaded her way through the shoppers on the other side of the street. Then he saw her again and his heart began to thump wildly. She was wearing a pale lemon, floaty dress, above which her long dark hair, curling deliciously at the ends, swung and shone in the sunlight. She radiated cool, healthy vigour as those around her seemed to wilt and melt in the July heat wave, so that he wondered why heads weren't turning to admire her as she went. He couldn't see her face clearly, but he recognised the way she walked: long-legged and purposeful, as if life was too full and too much fun to dawdle. As she turned into the arcade she tossed her head to flick the hair from her eyes in a way he remembered so well that he caught his breath.

His first instinct was to close the shop and run

after her, but Barbara, his assistant, would be back any minute from her lunch break and would wonder where he was. There was only one way in and out of the arcade, so if he stopped where he was he would see her again when she emerged.

He moved to the bay window from where he could get a better view, his heart still beating rapidly almost in time to the words repeating themselves in his head – *she's back! ... she's back!* Would she come out of the arcade and cross the road to his shop as she had done all those years ago?

As he waited, he turned his mind back...

She had bounded into the shop late one Saturday; a misty, damp autumn afternoon when few people were about. Dressed in a duffel coat that looked several sizes too big for her, and a bright red scarf wound round her neck, she oozed vitality. Her eye had been caught by a small lustre jug in the window.

"How much is the jug?" She had tossed her hair back then, and looked up at him with deep blue eyes.

"Ten pounds."

She had given a little grimace and then nodded her head in thanks before beginning to prowl around the shop. Alexander watched her, noticing how her reactions to her surroundings were reflected in the variety of expressions that flitted across her face. She studied this, picked up that, her hands absently caressing the smooth patina of chairs and tables as she squeezed round and past them, but all the time her eyes returned to the lustre jug.

On impulse he said, "I could reduce the jug."

He picked it off the window shelf and turned it around in his hands, "The flowers around the rim are hand-painted, but it's not of any particular significance."

She took the jug from him. Her fingers were slim and warm, despite the cold afternoon. "I think it was painted with great love by an impoverished young potter for his beautiful wife as they sat round the fire on an afternoon just like this one."

She had smiled at him then, inviting him to share in her flight of fancy, and he had smiled back.

"I could let you have it for seven pounds," he heard himself say, when he had been going to say eight.

The smile spread into a grin. "I think I can just about manage that! Done!"

He wrapped the jug and waited while she counted out six pound coins and then rummaged in the bottom of her purse for loose change to make up the rest, until there was nothing left in the purse.

"There! Just made it!" Her face glowed as she smiled at him again, triumphantly, and he was already lost. She buried her face in the folds of her scarf and turned to go, the jug clasped firmly to her.

"Is it a present for someone?" He wanted to keep her there, to find out more about her.

She looked at him impishly from under her dark fringe. "Yes – me! I'm studying Art History and Ceramics at the university – second year – and we've just finished a large assignment. I decided I needed a treat, and I've had my eye on this little jug for ages." Her eyes swept over the shop. "You have some lovely pieces here."

"Yes." It was all he could think of to say. Suddenly, from his lofty thirty years to her possible nineteen or twenty, he felt tongue-tied and gauche, and very, very, staid. "Do call again and look around. There's no obligation to buy."

The words sounded dry and formal to his own ears, but she smiled at him once more. "Thank you. I will."

The jangle of the shop doorbell broke into his thoughts as Barbara arrived, weighed down with shopping bags. Exceedingly stout, with greying hair that always managed to escape from the bun it was twisted into each morning, and beset with chiffon scarves and gold chains and bracelets, there seemed to be always some part of her that was moving. Now, tendrils of hair clung damply to her glowing face and her ample bosom heaved with the exertion of hurrying through her lunch-break.

"Oh! I'm so sorry I'm late Alexander! Were you waiting for me? You'll be wanting to get away!" She kicked the door gently behind her, and went to deposit her shopping bags in the tiny office at the back of the shop.

"No, it's all right, Barbara," Alexander replied absently, his eyes still on the arcade entrance, "I don't think I'll bother just yet." Better to wait and see whether she intends to come over here after the arcade.

Barbara turned in the office doorway. "But I thought you wanted to grab a sandwich before you go to the sale? I could have brought you one back if I'd thought."

He turned his head towards her. "What? Oh! Yes! The sale... I'd forgotten. Perhaps I'd better..." He glanced anxiously across the road again, and then went to pick up his briefcase. Perhaps he would just have time to look for her in the arcade before he set off for the sale.

"Let me know if anyone calls... I mean, if there are any messages, or, well... anything really, won't you?"

Barbara watched in surprise as her normally articulate, well-organised boss beat a flustered retreat out of the shop and hurried across the road. What had got into him? She shrugged her plump shoulders. No doubt she would find out if she were patient.

She saw the sale invoice for the button-back chair and went to fetch a 'Sold' label, whilst deciding how to rearrange the furniture once the chair was gone. She had a real love for her job, and dusted and arranged the antiques as if they were in her own sitting room. When the shop was quiet she filled out competitions in magazines with relentless enthusiasm, despite only ever winning minor prizes.

Alexander entered the arcade with a beating heart and dry mouth. What would he say to her when he found her? What would she say to him? Perhaps – dreadful thought – she was married. He strode rapidly from one shop to another, peering in through the doorways and bow windows that made up each old-fashioned unit. At one, a hairdresser's, he stared so long and so hard lest he should miss her amongst the driers and basins, that an assistant eventually stood on the other side of the glass and outstared him, until, realising, and flushing with embarrassment, he quickly moved away.

Eventually he had to admit defeat. She wasn't there. She must have slipped out of the arcade in the few moments it had taken him to gather his belongings and leave the shop. Dispirited, he made for his parked car and tried to turn his attention to the sale he was due to attend.

He edged into the one-way system, drumming his fingers on the steering wheel, not at the slow-moving traffic, but with frustration that he couldn't stay and search the whole town until he found her. He toyed with the idea of not going to the sale, but the catalogue had included a set of Jacobean dining chairs which he had promised to bid for on behalf of a customer.

At the end of the High Street he stopped suddenly, causing a van driver behind him to brake sharply and mouth incoherent obscenities at him through the windscreen. But Alexander didn't even notice. He had seen a swirl of lemon dress go through a department store door, and had tried in vain to see if it were her.

Moving off again, he was struck by a welcome thought. Perhaps she was waiting until the end of the afternoon, just as she had done in the old days, and when he got back she would waltz in through the shop door as if she had never been away.

Spurred on by this hope he accelerated away down the little winding lanes that led to the country house where the sale was to be held, as if, by travelling faster, he could speed up the afternoon itself and be back to welcome her into the shop.

As he drove, his mind was full of the past...

She had returned to the shop, as she had promised, a couple of weeks later, greeting him with the news that she had passed her assignment as if he were already an old friend.

"Congratulations! That's wonderful!" he had replied, drinking in the sight of her happy shining face. "What happens next?"

She gave a tiny shrug. "Finish this year, then one more at least, maybe two – exams – and then find a job, although I'm not sure where or what."

She leaned towards him, her hair swinging forward, so that he caught a waft of delicate perfume. She spoke in confidential tones. "What I'd really like to do is to join one of the big auction houses, and become an expert in ceramics – but of course, there are lots of other people who'd like to do that too, and I'm not nearly good enough, so I don't mention it to many people."

He smiled in appreciation of being trusted with her ambition. "I was just going to put the kettle on. Do you fancy a coffee to celebrate your success?"

As they waited for the kettle to boil, they walked around the shop together, discussing the items on sale.

"Are you the 'A. Russell' whose name is over the door?" she asked as she nursed her mug of coffee.

"Not exactly. That was my uncle, although I was named 'Alexander' after him. He had no children, and doted on me for some reason, taught me all he knew about antiques, and then left me the shop when he died."

"Wow! Some uncle! 'Alexander Russell' – sounds like a famous writer, or something." She solemnly held out her hand. "I'm Jo – Jo Hall – nowhere near as exciting-sounding, and it's short for Josephine."

He took her hand, warm like before, and fine-boned. Then she had smiled at him and tilted her head to one side. "I think, now that we're to be friends, that you'll have to be 'Alex'. What do you think?"

And he, who had steadfastly insisted on being called Alexander all his life, had smiled back and said, "I think that sounds fine."

Normally he would have enjoyed a sale of this type enormously, especially one so close to home. But as he strode into the fine old house he didn't notice the impressive facade, or the beautiful grounds basking in the sunshine; he was still preoccupied with the past.

"You have the serious air of a man who is going to spend a lot of money this afternoon," purred a voice behind him.

He turned round. "Oh, hello Vinny. I thought I'd see you here."

She tucked her hand in his arm. "And I was hoping to see you. I've a delicious picnic in the back of the car for later, with some very cold wine."

He patted her hand rather absently. "That sounds wonderful, but I shan't be staying long, I'm afraid. A few business things on the go at the moment. I'm only going to bid for the dining chairs."

Davinia Longworth regarded Alexander through narrowed eyes as they took their seats in the galleried hall. A stunningly attractive woman, who knew she looked good in the well-cut, understated but extremely expensive suits that she wore, she had long cherished hopes of developing a relationship with Alexander that went beyond the realms of antique auctions and art galleries. Now in her early thirties, there were times when desperation added a steely glint to her eye and made her beautifully sculpted smile a little harder.

A frustrating man, she thought, casting sideways glances at Alexander as the bidding began. Tall, dark, slim, with a whimsical air and a detachment that she longed to excite; and at times she thought she was succeeding, but then he would seem to withdraw again – just as he was doing to-day.

Unaware of his companion's exasperation, Alexander was remembering the way a slender warm hand would slip into his and squeeze it tightly when the bidding became exciting. Jo's Saturday visits to the shop had become increasingly frequent, until it was the natural thing to do to spend the evening together as well, and before long they were inseparable. Whenever she could she would accompany him to sales and auctions, convinced each time that they were going to make the find of the century, and laughing ruefully at herself when she insisted on bidding for some worthless piece of junk that she had nevertheless fallen for.

Alexander often worried that he was too old and set in his ways for her, but she would teasingly tell him that she enjoyed being an older man's plaything, and with relief he would put aside the nagging thought that she would have more fun with people her own age, and let the matter drop.

In pride of place on Jo's mantelpiece, in the house she shared with an ever-changing permutation of other students, stood the little lustre jug.

"My good luck charm," she told Alexander. "If I hadn't seen the jug, we would never have met."

The other students accepted Alexander with casual good grace, despite his 'straight' appearance and the sometimes pained expression that crossed his face at the clutter and general noisiness of their lives. The only times he felt truly at odds with them was when they were discussing their future; they were so full of bright ideas and plans for what they intended doing, and the places they wanted to see, and at these times Jo's voice was as eager as anyone else's. Alexander watched her, and cherished each day he spent with her, because he knew there would come a time when he would have to let her go...

"And now Lot 17: a set of six Jacobean dining chairs..."

He caught the words just in time to give a quick glance around the room to see who was likely to outbid him, and forced himself to deal with the matter in hand. A new kind of excitement began to rise in him. As soon as this was over he could return to the town. He was now convinced that Jo had returned, as she had said she would, and this time he wouldn't let her go again.

As soon as he had secured the chairs, he rose to leave. "'Bye, Vinny. I'll be in touch." He gave her an avuncular pat on the shoulder, and before she could comment on the strange light in is eye, he was gone.

Driving back, he was suddenly acutely aware of the

colour of the sky, the beauty of the countryside, the hedgerow brimming with buttercups and cow parsley. It was all as it had been that last, long summer when she had been preparing for her finals. Evening after evening they had sat by the riverbank, surrounded by text books, and when it had rained they had retired to his flat above the shop, because it was quieter than her house. When she was too tired to do any more he had held her in his arms, but he had never wanted to discuss what would happen once she had her degree. She was good, he knew that, and he wasn't going to stand in the way of the ambition she had shared with him right at the beginning, but he didn't want to face it until he had to.

The fateful day had arrived a few weeks after they had celebrated her honours degree by becoming gloriously, unashamedly drunk. She had come into the shop one morning, an envelope in her hand, and had stood quietly by the window until he had finished serving some customers, her face pale and serious.

"I've had an offer," she said, without preamble. "From the V. & A. To start next month."

"Why, that's wonderful!" he replied, trying hard to inject the enthusiasm into his voice that he had been privately practising for weeks.

"Yes. I – I think I should take it... unless... if you..."

She was gazing up at him, her eyes so dark they were almost black, steadfast and beseeching, so that he wanted to pull her into his arms and beg her to marry him, work with him, become his partner, anything as long as she would stay.

"Of course you should take it!" His voice seemed very loud in the stillness of the shop. "It's just the sort of opening you wanted... with the sort of experience you'll get there, you'll be running an auction house before you know it!"

He wished a customer, or Barbara, would come in and break the tension that hung in the air between them. Jo's head had drooped as he spoke, and for a moment or two she said nothing. Then she slowly raised her head and smiled a purposely bright smile, although her eyes now looked suspiciously watery.

"You're right! And I can come back every weekend… you won't get rid of me that easily, you know!"

The day before she left for London she solemnly handed him the lustre jug.

"I want you to have it. To look after it for me. Then I'll have to come back again, to claim it."

For a while she had come back almost every weekend. The lustre jug now sat on Alexander's mantelpiece, and she would smile at it and say that she was glad he was taking care of it. But gradually the visits became less frequent, as London life wrapped itself around her, as he had known it would, and eventually she had stopped coming back at all.

Three years, he mused, as he parked the car. Three years to get everything she wanted to do out of her system, and now she had returned.

"Goodness, you're back early!" Barbara jangled towards him as he entered the shop. "You needn't have bothered – it's been fairly quiet, although I've sold some bits of china to a couple of Americans…"

For a moment he was stricken. Jo hadn't come to the shop. Then he realised. Of course! She would be coming back to claim the jug! She had never returned her key to the flat. She would be there, waiting to surprise him!

Without a word, he turned, leaving a puzzled Barbara open-mouthed, and hurried to the door round the corner, which led up to his flat. But that was empty too. The lustre jug was on the mantelpiece, where it had been for three years, and the only sound was the ticking of the clock in the hall. He went from room to room, and only just stopped himself from futilely calling out her name.

She hadn't come.

He walked over to the window that overlooked the street, his spirits sinking as rapidly as they had soared earlier in the day. He stayed there for some time, unwilling to return to the shop and what he knew would be Barbara's barely concealed curiosity.

The loneliness of the last three years swept over him. Perhaps now was the time to cut his losses, admit that she wasn't going to come back, and make the best of it. He knew that Davinia was there for him if he wanted. Perhaps, if he put Jo firmly and finally out of his mind, their friendship might stand a chance of becoming something more.

Suddenly and instantly his resolve was shattered. He saw her again! She was walking down the road towards the bus station, the lemon dress a deeper yellow in the afternoon sun. He stayed only for a moment to be sure of what he was seeing. Of course it was Jo! Her face, her body, her movements, were etched so firmly on his mind that he would recognise her anywhere.

Then a further thought struck him. The bus station! Perhaps she had returned and then had been unable to pluck up the courage to come to him after all this time, and now she was leaving again!

He couldn't let it happen. Within seconds he was back in the street, dodging the traffic to cross the road, his mind swirling. He would beg her to stay! They could go for dinner somewhere quiet and talk. He would tell her that it didn't matter that she had been away so long; they could start again.The streets were still busy with shoppers and tourists, and for the moment he couldn't see her, but he was sure he knew where she was heading. His long legs soon covered the distance between them as he edged past shoppers or darted into the road to skirt round them.

Now he could see her! He increased his pace until he was running, not caring any more as he jostled shopping bags and bumped into prams. As he neared her he could almost smell her perfume and feel the softness of her skin. He covered the last couple of yards and stretched out his hand to touch her shoulder. All he could say was, "Jo!"

She turned at his touch. A pair of sensible brown eyes looked with faint surprise into his. His hand recoiled. "Oh! Oh, I'm sorry! I thought…"

The stranger smiled at him; a slight, impersonal acknowledgement, and then she turned and walked on.

It was nearly dark in the flat, but still he sat, too wrapped in misery to turn on the lights, or even to give up and go to bed. He had gone back to the shop eventually, and poured out the full extent of his woe to Barbara, who had clucked and jangled and consoled until he almost couldn't bear it.

The ringing of the doorbell broke into his thoughts. He sighed. Probably Barbara had telephoned Davinia and urged her to keep him company. Well, he wasn't in the mood for Vinny's sort of company. If he ignored it, she would think he was in bed.

But it rang again, and his innate good manners told him that he should answer it. He went wearily down the stairs and opened the street door, his eyes cast down as he prepared his excuses.

On the pavement was a lumpy hold-all, next to which was a pair of bare feet in sandals. His gaze travelled upwards, past a floaty lemony dress, to long dark hair, curling deliciously at the ends, and a pair of deep blue eyes above an impish grin.

"I've come to claim my jug," she said.

Just Like James

The first surprise was the cottage. It wasn't a bit like I had imagined. In my mind's eye it had been rose-covered and topped by thatch, but here it was, one of a pair, built of uncompromising red brick with a slate roof, and sharing an area of rough grass with barely a flower in sight.

The second surprise was the goose, which came honking round from the back of the house to stand squarely in front of the gate, wings flapping threateningly and hissing fiercely so that, laden with suitcase and bags, I hesitated to lift the catch.

"Jemima! Stand back girl!" A firm, deep voice came from the back of the cottages, and soon its owner appeared, giving me the third, and least welcome, surprise. He advanced towards me; tall, with honey-blond hair flopping forward slightly over his brow, beneath which was a pair of green eyes set in an extremely handsome face. His smile was confident, charming. He was... *just like James!*

"Don't mind Jemima," he said, patting the goose on the head so that she immediately calmed down and moved away. "She's an excellent protector – better than a guard dog any day."

"I know Jemima is supposed to be a puddle duck," he went on as he opened the gate, presumably taking my bemused silence for continued misgivings about the creature, "but I couldn't think of what a goose is supposed to be called, except 'Mother', and that didn't seem right somehow!"

He took my bags from me and ushered me into the garden with another winning smile that made my heart lurch. At the cottage door, Jemima eyeing us malevolently from a distance, he put the bags down and offered his hand.

"Simon Ellis, estate agent from Exeter. I'm spending a few weeks doing up next door so that I can rent it out for holidays."

"Caroline Hunt," I answered faintly, aware that he was holding on to my hand for rather longer than was necessary while his eyes roved approvingly over me. "I'm a writer. I'm here to do some research for a book... farm life... that sort of thing... Rachel's lent me the cottage..."

I managed to stop babbling and he let go of my hand.

"Well, I don't know a thing about farm life, except that the wretched cockerel wakes us all up at a disgustingly early hour, but if ever you're suffering from writer's block and need a diversion, let me know!"

I stuttered my thanks, refused his offer to help me settle in, dragged my bags into the cottage, and thankfully closed the door.

The cottage was a lot more welcoming inside, with a pretty sitting room dominated by a large Victorian fireplace. At the far end, opening onto the garden, were French windows, in front of which was a sturdy table, ideal for working on. Beyond the sitting room was a small kitchen, with well-stocked cupboards and an old-fashioned gas stove. It was really quite charming, but I was no longer in the mood to appreciate it. As soon as I'd made myself a coffee, I fished out my phone and called Rachel.

"Oh! Is Simon there?" Rachel's voice was deliberately casual, which didn't fool me for one minute. "Well at least you won't feel lonely – after all, you're not really used to the country, are you?"

"But Rachel!" I wailed, "he's just like James!" Witty,

captivating James, who had kept me on a string for longer than I cared to admit. James, who had turned out to be a complete philanderer and left me heartbroken. The main reason for my retreat to Rachel's cottage was to heal my torn emotions and recover the shattered remnants of my self-respect.

"I suppose he is a bit like James," Rachel was saying now, as if the likeness had only just occurred to her. 'Never mind. You'll be at the farm a lot of the time, and when you're not you'll be busy with your book, won't you?"

A pointed reminder that, as well as being my best friend, Rachel was also my agent and the hours spent shedding tears over James had left my current effort way behind schedule.

I spent the rest of the afternoon and evening unpacking and cooking myself a comfort meal, of all the things I loved but I knew weren't good for me.

Once my laptop and paper and pencils were set out on the sitting room table my spirits began to rise. Tomorrow I would throw myself into my research and I wouldn't even think about the man next door with tantalising green eyes, *just like...*

ℕext morning I rose just after the cockerel had begun to crow, donned my new blue dungarees which I had deemed were just right for working in the country, tied my hair back, and ate my breakfast watching the countryside come to life through the kitchen window. Having made sure Jemima was at the far end of the back garden, I hurried out of the front and set off to meet Michael, the farmer.

Although his was a modern dairy farm, he kept a corner of it just as it had been in the 'good old days' with a variety of animals cared for by old-fashioned means, and it was this that really interested me. This part of the farm was open to the public in the afternoons, Michael had explained to me in his emails, and played a vital financial part in keeping the rest of the farm going.

Michael turned out to be younger than I had imagined from his messages, his welcome warm and friendly and tinged by a soft Devon burr. He took me into the large farmhouse kitchen and introduced me to his housekeeper, Annie Armitage, who nodded and eyed my pristine dungarees dourly.

"I think there's some boots in the wash-house that'll fit," was all she said.

"What would you like me to tell you about first?" Michael asked as we set off towards the cow-sheds.

"I don't exactly have a list of questions," I replied, noticing that he looked relieved that I wasn't going to follow him around with a notebook and pencil. "I just want to spend as much time as I can around the farm with you – helping if possible, although I'm a complete novice, – and perhaps you can tell me how your methods to-day compare with how your parents ran the farm."

He nodded. "Sounds fine by me. But you make sure you ask when you want to know something. Things are a bit busy hereabouts at this time of year, and I go a bit quiet when I've got a lot to think about."

'Busy' turned out to be a complete understatement. As well as caring for the dairy herd, Michael and his two farm hands were in the midst of summer haymaking, so that by the time we stopped for lunch I could hardly believe that it was only mid-day.

Lunch was eaten in the kitchen, under the watchful eye of Annie, who seemed to relent a little towards me when she saw that my dungarees were now dirty.

In the afternoon, Michael found the time to show me round the old farm corner which, being a week-day, hadn't many visitors. He answered all my questions carefully and placidly, as if he had all the time in the world.

"This is Mildred," he said, patting the rump of a beautiful Jersey cow. "We show all our visitors how to hand-milk her, and the good old girl never lets us down." With that he pulled up a stool and gave me a demonstration.

"Now you try," he said.

I gave a whoop of satisfaction as my first attempt produced a gush of milk, which changed to a flush of dismay when I realised that I had missed the bucket and squirted milk down Michael's trouser-leg.

"Don't you worry!" he said, with a grin which lit up his dark features. "You did very well for a first go."

A corner of the barn was set out with old household and farm implements. Michael pointed to a butter churn. "Old Annie can still make butter by hand." He winked solemnly at me. "You get on the right side of her and she'll show you."

Late afternoon found me dragging myself back to the cottage, amazed that Michael and his workers still had the energy to face evening milking. All I felt like facing was a warm shower followed by a cool drink in the garden.

But I had forgotten about Jemima. This time I did manage to get through the gate before she came rushing up, preventing me from taking a step forward, and once again Simon had to come to my rescue.

"Good day mucking out the cow-sheds?" he asked, raising one eyebrow, and surveying me with amusement, so that I suddenly became aware of what a state I must look.

"Very good," I replied, lifting my chin to show I didn't care.

"Then how about supper with me to celebrate your first day?"

Memories of candlelit suppers with James and being held in his arms afterwards came flooding over me, and Simon was *so like James...*

"No thank you," I forced myself to say, ignoring the slight quiver in my voice. "I'm really very tired."

"Okay," he shrugged, with the easy air of a man who knows that he cannot be resisted for long. I edged past Jemima, who looked as if she was longing to nip my leg, and fled into the cottage, where I spent the entire evening taking out my feelings on the keyboard, until weariness completely overcame me.

I had planned to spend part of each day at the farm, and the rest in the cottage, setting down my impressions while they were still fresh, but it was not that easy. Whenever I settled down to work, Simon would appear in the garden, seemingly doing all sorts of things with a saw and bits of wood, so that my concentration would be shattered. Often I would look up and he would wave and smile that devastating smile, or appear at the French doors with a cup of coffee and a suggestion as to how we should spend the rest of the day.

So I took to spending more and more time at the farm. After a while my presence seemed to be accepted by everyone, and I joined in the farm routine with a willingness that surprised me. Michael became a good friend; the sort who invites confidences without sitting in judgement.

One day I found myself telling him all about James. We were sharing a picnic lunch in the furthest field from the farm, overlooking a breathtakingly beautiful valley.

Michael listened in his unhurried way. "I was engaged once," he said, staring out across the countryside. "But it didn't come to anything. She was a city-type girl, and I was too buried in the country down here for her liking."

I understood what he meant. It was the sort of hot still day when nothing seemed to be moving. City life and publishers' deadlines seemed a world away.

I even made some headway with Annie, and sometimes in the afternoon, reluctant to return to the cottage, I would sit in the kitchen with her, drinking tea. I mentioned Simon to her, and how attractive he was. She had seen him in the village, but she only sniffed.

"Handsome is as handsome does," she said enigmatically, and refused to discuss him after that.

The evenings gave me more opportunity to write. I would hear Simon's front door bang and then the roar of his car engine as he shot up the bumpy lane, and I would know some peace. Still not much writing was done, though. Before long the screen on the laptop would begin to blur and my eyelids start to droop.

Nearly two weeks after my arrival I heard Simon's door bang early in the evening, but instead of his car engine it was followed by a tap on my own front door.

"You've been here almost a fortnight," he said, striding masterfully into the sitting room, "and not one evening out! I'm meeting some friends down at the local – come and join us! They've stopped believing my tales of my beautiful new neighbour."

He was wearing a white shirt which showed off his tan, and the room was filled with the smell of expensive after-shave. Weak-kneed and weak-willed, I tried to prevaricate. "But I'm not ready... I'll have to change..." I was dressed in old jeans and a faded T-shirt.

"You look fine as you are – it's only the local."

Persuaded, I ran upstairs to flick a comb through my hair, put on some lipstick, and a quick spray of perfume.

A crowd of Simon's friends had already filled the small saloon bar. They were go-ahead young men from Exeter and glamorous girls who instantly made me wish I had changed after all. Simon put his arm possessively round my waist as he introduced me, but he didn't offer to find me a seat, so we stood, his hand caressing me absently, as if he knew how easily I would succumb to his charms, while he quickly became the life and soul of the party. He was obviously popular with the girls, who hung on his words and laughed long at his jokes.

It was all so reminiscent of evenings I had spent with James that I found my attention wandering. Across the room you could see into the public bar. Michael was there, talking to three other men. As I recognised him, he lifted his head and caught my eye. He looked thoughtfully at me for a moment, and then, with the merest hint of a smile, raised his glass in salute.

Simon's friends came back to his cottage at closing time, the girls giggling in the dark, and shrieking when Jemima loomed up in front of them. Pleading an early start next day, I headed for my own front door, largely unnoticed because everyone was trying to get away from the goose.

"I know Jemima is supposed to be a puddle duck..." I heard Simon say as I turned my key in the door. Once in bed, though, sleep eluded me, and not only because of the noise coming through the wall.

"You should have stayed in bed," Michael said sympathetically when I dragged myself over to the farm next morning.

"But I like the early morning milking," I replied, and smiled at him as it dawned on me that I meant it. After that the day became brighter.

I returned home just after lunch, determined to get down to work. But soon Simon appeared through the French window.

"Good time last night, wasn't it?" he said, "You should have stayed with us afterwards – sorry if we were a bit noisy."

I murmured that it didn't matter, and he stepped nearer.

"How about dinner tonight, just the two of us?" He lifted his hand and caressed the side of my face. "There's a very romantic little restaurant I know not far from here."

His nearness, the seductiveness of his voice, his green eyes, *so much like James.*

"I'll think about it... I'm awfully behind with my writing... I'll let you know later..."

He smiled, and kissed me lightly on the cheek. "I'll come round this evening," he murmured huskily.

After he had gone I fled to the farm. I had become quite practiced at milking Mildred, and suddenly I wanted to lean my head against her warm side. I needed to think. Michael found me there some time later, still talking to Mildred about what I should do.

At about seven o' clock that evening Simon came into the cottage. His eyes lit up appreciatively as he saw me. I was wearing the only decent dress I had brought with me, a flirty little black number, and I was carefully made up, with my freshly-washed hair piled on top of my head in a style that I knew suited me.

He smiled broadly. "You've decided then!"

I could see the glow of satisfaction in his eyes as he moved further into the room. I had seen it before, in James, whenever he thought he had made a conquest.

"Yes, I've decided," I replied, confident now that I knew his charm could have no more effect on me, "and I'm afraid I can't go out with you this evening – I've had another invitation." I turned at the front door and smiled happily. "Must go. Lock the door behind you when you leave, won't you?"

I knew he was watching me as I walked down the path, blithely ignoring the hissing Jemima, to where Michael was waiting for me, dark and dashingly handsome in his best grey suit.

Steadfast, gentle Michael, who knew that the best way to mend a girl's broken heart was to be patient, kind and loving.

Not a bit like James.

Lost and Found

*I*t didn't stop dramatically, with an explosive discharge, or hissing of escaping steam. As Lizzie manoeuvred her car along the meandering lane, the engine simply juddered a few times before fizzling to a halt.

"Oh no!" she groaned. "How could you do this to me – here! – now ! – of all times?"

Her nerves were already tightly-drawn from forty-five minutes of hopelessly turning down one hedge-lined road after another, until they all seemed part of a tangled web from which she would never escape.

The car wheezed and spluttered but persistently refused to do more in response to Lizzie's turning of the ignition.

"You were only serviced a few weeks ago!" she said accusingly, releasing the bonnet catch and taking a torch from the glove compartment.

She really had no idea what to look for, but it was what one was supposed to do when broken down, and a small, optimistic part of her thought the answer might be glaringly obvious. Technical terms used by men in pubs, such as spark plugs and alternators, popped into her brain, but she couldn't locate any of these marvels, let alone know if they were causing the problem.

Cursing mildly, she replaced the bonnet and tried the engine again. Nothing. Not even a geriatric, phlegmy cough. What now? If she had even the faintest idea where she was she would walk, but Steve's directions had long since been flung across the passenger seat alongside her flat mobile.

But it was no good just sitting here. She would walk to the next bend in the hope of at least finding a house with a telephone she could use.

But the next bend produced nothing new; just a further expanse of tree-lined lane bordering fields stretching on indefinitely.

She turned to re-trace her footsteps, aware suddenly of the closing in of the light; and with it the lane became a narrow claustrophobic tunnel. The trees, just an hour earlier having thrilled her with their early summer mantle of fresh green, now were dark, brooding and sinister, their untamed branches reaching menacingly towards her as if to pull her irrevocably into their rustic web. The still air was cooler, and although one or two birds continued to sing as if reluctant to concede that the day was over, their songs held plaintiveness – or even a warning.

The romantic, sun-strewn, picture-book countryside of benign cattle and gambolling lambs was giving way to the harsh reality of a hostile environment where the nocturnal habits of a score of different animals involved the stealthy pursuit of the helpless by the strong...

Absorbed in quelling her rising panic, she didn't hear any footsteps as she reached the car. So when a hand tapped her shoulder she let out a piercing scream.

"I'm sorry, I didn't mean to startle you." The man's voice was gentle and cultured, the sort of voice you always hoped your family doctor would have, but still she pulled away from his hand before turning to face him. He was tall and very thin, with straggly brown hair and large, hooded eyes which made him appear rather cadaverous. In contrast his teeth, when he gave a reas-suring smile, gleamed white and even.

"Where did you come from?" she demanded, her voice high and strained, as she searched the lane for a vehicle.

"I saw you were in trouble," he answered. "Can I help?"

Garbled fragments of stories of women found strangled and mutilated in dark country lanes crowded into her head. Yet it would be foolish to pretend everything was all right and send him away.

"I'm supposed to be visiting friends near here but my stupid car has broken down." She kept her voice firm to show she wasn't scared. "I should have arrived ages ago – they'll have organised a search party by now."

"I know a bit about engines. Shall I look while you wait for your friends?" The voice again. Deep and honeyed. Not the voice of a man crazed with lust and violent thoughts.

He was waiting for her answer. If she didn't turn her back on him... if he really could fix the car, she could drive off very quickly, before there was time for him to grab her...

She pulled herself together. "Okay. Thanks."

"So if you'll just open the bonnet?"

At least he wasn't patronising, Lizzie decided, as she sat once more in the car and released the catch. Not like some men who say "Let me try" and move into the driver's seat, as if their turning of the ignition key would make all the difference, and then say, "No, it won't start," as if you didn't know that all along.

But then rapists wouldn't need to patronise you over something as mundane as a car engine. They'd have other ways of humiliating women.

She jumped again when he tapped on the window. "It's getting a bit dark. Do you have a torch?"

She meekly handed him the instrument with which he would probably bludgeon her to death – after or before he raped her? He appeared to weigh it in his hand for a second before asking, "And a tool kit?"

With a nice big spanner in it. To do the job more swiftly and satisfyingly. Perhaps she should engage him in conversation, she decided as she fetched the kit from the boot – hadn't she read somewhere that it was harder to murder someone with whom you'd struck up a rapport?

"Do you live near here?" She used her bright, social voice.

His lean body was bent over the engine from which came a series of taps and clunks. "Quite near."

She couldn't think of anything more to say. In the encroaching darkness she could smell the earthy aroma of damp ditches and banks. *It could take weeks before a body was discovered in a place like this, perhaps not even dead at first...*

Stop it! she told herself. *This is ridiculous! You're just overwrought and irrational!* But nightfall was only serving to increase the sensation of being marooned in an alien, unrecognisable place, isolated from contact with any other human being except this man.

She looked at his hands as they tinkered. Long, tapering fingers – *fingers that might caress and embrace before exerting a gradual deadly pressure on the most sensitive part of the neck...*

He straightened up, handing her the torch. "I think that may have done the trick. Just a loose connection. Try it again."

She shone the torch full in his face. If he left her alive she wanted to be able to recount his features. The hooded eyes looked back at her, dark and unfathomable, yet seeming to know everything in her mind.

"Thank you," she said. "I'm really most grateful – sorry if I've held you up."

His eyes followed her as she bumbled her way back into the car, and she was struck by their kindness. Surely killer eyes didn't look kind?

Relief as the engine started immediately made her smile up at him through the open window.

"Wonderful... I can't thank you enough... I'd better be going..."

He leaned into the window, obliterating what little light remained. "Sure you know the way?" Concern deepened his voice further and for a moment she wished she'd met him somewhere more ambient.

"Of course," she lied, "it's just after this road."

She felt rather than saw his half-smile. "You do know this is a dead-end? Are you, perhaps, lost?"

With a resigned air she handed over Steve's scrunched-up directions. "They're called Steve and Jane Elliott. Mile End Cottage. Do you know it?"

Ignoring the creased paper he nodded. "Yes, but you're quite a way out. I'd better take you there."

Before she could protest he'd climbed into the passenger seat. "You'll have to turn round and go back up this lane. Left at the top."

She jumped as he put his hand in his jacket pocket. She tightened her grip on the steering wheel. *Now it was going to happen! He was going to bring out a six-inch knife and slit her throat while she was strapped into her seat. She could already feel the coldness of the blade against her skin which would be swiftly followed by a warm, sticky trickle – or even a gush – of her own blood...*

He caught her movement and slowed his own, carefully extracting his handkerchief.

"Oily fingers," he explained, wiping his hands. After a pause he said, "You really mustn't be afraid of me. I'm not going to hurt you. I'm only here to help. Take the right fork just after this bend."

Her voice was a little too high as she answered. "Of course I'm not afraid of you. It's... it's just... well, I don't usually give rides to strange men in my car... not that you're strange, of course..." *What was she doing risking antagonising him?* "I just mean, well, I don't even know your name... Mine's Lizzie, by the way."

"How do you do?" he answered gravely. "I'm... Chris." His smile again, flashing white in the darkness. "Does that make you feel better?"

She laughed, more naturally. "Much".

They drove on, down endless dark burrows illuminated only by the car's headlights. Suddenly, there was a rabbit, crouching compactly in the middle of the road, hypnotised by the glare of the lights. Lizzie cried out as she slammed on the brakes, but still the rabbit huddled, its coat paling in the harsh spotlight. She pulled the steering wheel hard left, grazing the bank as the engine stalled, bringing them to a sudden halt.

"It's all right, it's all right," he soothed her as she leaned over the wheel. "You missed it. It's run off. It's all right."

His hand on her shoulder radiated warmth through her thin top. She no longer felt afraid. She glanced up, into the heavy-lidded eyes. The warmth seared her whole body and she knew with complete conviction that to be loved by this man would be greater than anything she'd ever known. She yearned to lean against his shoulder and have his arms encompass her.

"Not far now," he said quietly. "Your journey's nearly over."

She straightened in her seat and swung the car back out onto the narrow road. She didn't want it to end now. Now, she wanted to stay with him in this snug cocoon, immune from the outside world. It couldn't end. She'd invite him in for some food and drink, while she, in turn, fed her hunger to know more of this man.

Around a final curve there was the cottage, its windows lit and welcoming.

"Won't you come in with me? They'll be so pleased to meet my rescuer." She felt diffident now, hesitating to raise her eyes to his.

"I'll see you to the door," he replied.

They stood at the gate of the old-fashioned garden. A sliver of moon had risen and the air was filled with the pungency of nearby honeysuckle. A cacophony of happy wine-enriched voices spewed from the open windows, into the silence.

"Come on," Lizzie said. "They'll have given up on me ever getting here."

The door was flung open at her first knock and there were her friends, smiling at her appearance.

"I got hopelessly lost, and then my car broke down," she told them lightheartedly, now all terrors were vanquished. "And then Chris here" – she indicated behind her – "appeared out of the blue, fixed the car and brought me here. So I said he must come in for a drink and... "

Her friends were looking past her, with puzzled faces. She turned.

"Chris?... Chris?" Her voice was as hoarse as if he had, indeed, tried to strangle her.

Shadows of spiky lupins rose over softer mounds of geraniums. The tang of honeysuckle was offset by the sweetness of an early rose. Everything was very still.

And he was gone.

The Sofa

It was no good, it would have to go. The love-hate relationship Sorrel had had with the sofa for months now was definitely veering more towards hate. It dominated her compact sitting room, and, more importantly, had come to symbolise everything that had gone wrong in her life. So, it would have to go.

She had loved it, of course, when she and Marcus had first bought it. Wide and deep, in a mellow gold fabric, with big squashy cushions and luxurious rolled arms, she and Marcus would have been foolish not to snap it up when they had seen it in the sale.

The two of them had sat on it night after night, making their plans, carried away by the dreams Sorrel was weaving for them. A natural country dweller, living in the city was for her simply a means to an end, a way to become sufficiently successful to make the dreams come true.

Marcus, born and bred in the town, was entranced with the pictures Sorrel conjured up. Inside their cottage would be a pine-clad kitchen with mellow red quarry tiles on the floor; there would be a small room where Sorrel could carry on designing, and a sunny lounge where the sofa would have pride of place.

"And in the garden we can grow hollyhocks and delphiniums – and herbs, of course," she told him.

"Including your namesake," Marcus had said. "I

wonder if that's why you have such an affinity with the countryside?"

"Well, remember my Mum was the original Seventies earth mother," she replied. "Be thankful that she didn't chose a name like 'Moonbeam' or goodness knows how I would have turned out!"

And Marcus had laughed and they had enfolded themselves in the depths of the sofa, their plans for the future momentarily forgotten in the immediacy of their love for one another.

Remembering, Sorrel eyed the sofa malevolently. Curled up alone in one corner of its vastness was a cold experience and she had spent many an evening convincing herself that the tears she was shedding were caused by nothing more than the soppy old film she had been watching on T.V.

So it would have to go, and she would get on with her life. It had been difficult, of course, after they broke up, with Marcus still living in his flat across the landing and they had carefully avoided each other for weeks. Now they existed in a sort of strained truce, briefly polite about nothing in particular if they happened to meet. Sorrel had considered holding on to the dream and moving to the country on her own, but somehow it was less appealing now.

She sat on a hard chair at the table drafting out an ad for the local paper, purposely avoiding glancing at the sofa as she did so, as if it would suddenly accuse her of betrayal. "This is ridiculous," she told herself, but kept her back to the sofa nonetheless.

The ad resulted in plenty of interest. Several people telephoned, and two or three came round to see it, each of whom shook their head and said doubtfully, "It is very big, isn't it?"

"Which is why the advertisement said 'large sofa'," Sorrel muttered through clenched teeth.

Finally a couple arrived who fell in love with it in the same way as Sorrel and Marcus had, and immediately struck a bargain, agreeing to collect it early the following evening. Even better, Sorrel thought. It will be gone before Marcus gets home from work. For some reason she didn't want to tell him that she was getting rid of it.

After the couple had gone, she looked at the sofa for some minutes, stroking its top absently. Selling it was almost like getting rid of a troublesome pet, she decided. You couldn't cope with it yourself, but wanted to make sure it went to a good home.

A good home. She allowed herself a final indulgence of remembering the dream. What had gone wrong? Admittedly searching for the ideal cottage in January hadn't been the best of ideas. There had been an awful lot of mud, and, seen through Marcus's eyes, perhaps the countryside did seem a mite depressing at that time of year.

And then his promotion had come at the same time, and he had jumped at it, even though it meant that he was away, travelling round the country, more often than he was home.

"But I'm doing it for us!" he had protested when Sorrel pointed out that they saw very little of each other any more. "You'll see, once we're married with our own special place, everything will be fine!"

But the opportunities to find their special place became less and less, as did the evenings snuggled up together on the sofa, so that it had only taken one bitter row – and she couldn't even remember what had started it now – for the dream finally to turn to dust.

"It'll take some shifting, that will." The little man who had driven the removal van sucked in his moustache and shook his head. "Would have brought my mate if I'd thought it was going to be difficult."

Twenty minutes later they were all wishing he had as the young couple, Sorrel, and the little man confused each other with conflicting instructions, which had resulted in the sofa becoming stuck in the doorway and then again on the bend in the stairs.

"The men who brought it didn't seem to have this

trouble," Sorrel remarked, and then wished she hadn't when the little man glared at her indignantly.

They had just reached the ground floor and all stood back to catch their breath when the front door opened and Marcus came in. He stared in surprise at the sofa and their four red faces – Sorrel's turning a slightly deeper shade than the rest. He wasn't supposed to be here yet. Trust him to pick today to be early for once.

"What's all this?" he demanded, in what seemed to Sorrel a bossy tone of voice, which made her bite back a sarcastic retort.

"It's the sofa, of course," she answered. "I'm selling it."

"Selling it? But you can't do that! It's our sofa!"

"*Was* our sofa," she corrected him. "And don't worry, I hadn't forgotten your share in it! I'll give you half the money!"

His eyes blazed as he towered above her, making her stomach churn as she was reminded of how attractive he looked in a business suit.

"That's not what I meant! The money doesn't matter. It's just that... we chose it together... it was special... you could have asked me first when you decided to sell it."

"I didn't think you were bothered about it any more."

"How would you know what I was bothered about when we've hardly spoken in weeks!"

"Well we're speaking now! Do you want it?"

"Yes... no... I can't... there isn't room for it in my flat."

"Exactly!" she exclaimed.

A small discreet cough from the little man with the moustache reminded them of the three other people who had been watching this exchange with the intentness of the crowd at a Wimbledon final.

"Can we get on?" the little man asked.

"Yes, of course, I'm sorry." Sorrel brushed past Marcus and opened the front door, holding it wide whilst the man and the young couple struggled to carry the sofa out to the van.

"Doesn't it mean anything to you?" Marcus hissed at her, coming to stand beside her as, with a final heave, the sofa disappeared inside the van.

"There isn't room in my flat, either," she hissed back, neatly sidestepping a direct answer to his question. "Anyway," she went on, "why are you here at this time? You're not usually back for hours!"

He looked ahead as the young couple gave a cheery wave and the van set off. "I've changed my job. No more travelling. Nine to five office hours from now on."

The van was disappearing up the road, carrying away all the hopes and dreams they had once had. Anger welled up inside Sorrel. Why couldn't he have done this when they were together?

"Well, that's just dandy!" she cried, slamming the front door as she turned towards him. "I hope you enjoy all the spare time you'll have from now on!"

He opened his mouth to speak, but she stomped off up the stairs and into her flat, determined not to let him see the tears that were threatening to spill over.

A long hot soak in the bath, Sorrel decided as she plodded up the path after work the next day. Then she would ring up her friend Jodie and suggest an evening out. Somehow, she couldn't face another evening in the flat. She had spent much of the previous one re-arranging the furniture to fill the gap left by the sofa, and convincing herself that she really was better off without it.

She turned the key in the front door and then gasped in astonishment. There, filling most of the entrance hall was the sofa. There was an envelope on the seat with a note inside which said, "Sorry, the sofa was too big for our place after all."

They could have called me, Sorrel thought, grappling in her bag for her mobile to check that she hadn't missed a call, *not just dumped it back on me like this. And what about the cash they'd given her?*

As she stood with the phone in her hand, the door to the bottom flat opened and Mrs. Flynn, caretaker to the building, came out. "You'll have to shift it," she said in her usual spare way. A small, thin woman, she reserved all her energy for cleaning the stairs down. "Been there all afternoon it has, almost blocking poor Mr. Allen's door. He'll have something to say when he gets in."

"But I can't get it back up the stairs on my own!" Sorrel protested, beginning to look round wildly in the hope that a couple of strong men might suddenly materialise from nowhere.

As if in answer to her prayers, there was a rap at the open front door and a voice said, "Excuse me!"

A tall genial young man wearing a dog collar stood in the doorway. "Sorry to interrupt you, but we're collecting for St. George's Youth Club Jumble Sale. Just wondered if you had anything..."

Out in the road stood an old, open-backed lorry.

On impulse, Sorrel indicated the sofa. "You can have this, if you can get it on the lorry."

The young vicar's eyes widened. "It's much too good for our jumble sale. But it would be great in the youth club coffee room. Are you sure you want us to have it?"

"Yes... yes I am, if you take it straight away," Sorrel said.

"Right. Many thanks." He called out through the door. "Come on lads!" And in no time at all he and three gangly youths had the sofa tied onto the back of the lorry and were away.

Mrs. Flynn nodded her approval at such a swift resolution to the problem and returned to her flat, just as Marcus burst through the front door, a distracted expression on his face.

"Was that the sofa on the back of that lorry?" he demanded without preamble.

"It was," Sorrel said wearily, wishing by now that she had never set eyes on that particular piece of furniture in the first place. "It's going to St George's Youth Club, for their coffee room."

"But... it can't be... the young couple from last night... I thought..." he stammered.

"They brought it back because it was too big. It was stuck in the hallway here and Mrs. Flynn was giving me grief, so I gave it to the vicar when he turned up asking for stuff for the youth club."

"But it will be ruined! There'll be chewing gum stuck on it, and great strapping lads in Doc Marten's will jump all over it!"

Sorrel shrugged, steeling herself not to share in his picture of the sofa's demise. "It doesn't matter. It's gone, that's the main thing."

Marcus moved swiftly in front of her, to bar her way as she went to climb the stairs.

"Would it matter if I told you that I changed my job in the hope that we could get back together again? That nothing has been the same since we split up, and that all I want is to go back to finding that place in the country?"

Sorrel stared at him solemnly, remembering how flecks of deeper colour would appear in his hazel eyes when he was deadly serious or excited about something. The flecks were there now.

"Would it matter?" he˜ persisted.

"It might," she said. They gazed at each other cautiously for a moment or two.

"Do you know where St. George's is?" he asked.

"At the bottom of Melrose Road, I think," she said.

He held out his hand. "Come on."

The sofa had already lost a castor, so that it had a slightly lopsided look, and there was a scuffmark near the bottom where it had been dragged across the bare floorboards. Marcus spent some minutes emptying notes out of his wallet as a donation to youth club funds, before the vicar, who drove a hard bargain for a man of the cloth, agreed to let them have it back.

"Do you think, for a further consideration, you could bring it back – now – on the lorry?" Marcus asked, waving another twenty pound note around.

They were watching the sofa being lifted off the lorry when a car pulled up behind, and out jumped the young woman of the night before. In her hand was the missing castor, which she handed to Marcus.

"This came off when you bought the sofa back," she said. Then she patted Sorrel's arm: "It did look quite nice in our place, but we understood in the end."

"Well, that's more than I do," Sorrel said, turning to Marcus as the woman went back to her car, muttering about holding up the traffic.

But Marcus had already hurried after the sofa which was being manhandled through the hallway by the youth club gang on the vicar's instructions. "Hang on a minute lads, I'll just put this on!"

Sorrel ran after him and grabbed his arm.

"I thought there was something familiar about the handwriting on that note!" she exclaimed. "What on earth did you do that for? I told you I had no room for it!"

He had the grace to look sheepish.

"It was all part of a plan I made last night," he confessed. "I was going to come home to find you there with the sofa, offer to help you to get it back upstairs, then persuade you that we really should keep it... tell you about my new job...and so on..."

Sorrel began to giggle. "You must have had such a shock when you saw it being carried off down the road again!"

Marcus chuckled. "You bet I did! And with what it's cost me to get it back – twice – we could almost have afforded another one!"

"It wouldn't have been the same, though, would it?" Sorrel said softly.

The dark flecks were back in his eyes. "No. It wouldn't."

The noise of the sofa being hauled up the stairs brought Mrs. Flynn to her door again. "What's going on now?" she asked.

But as the sofa disappeared round the bend in the stairs, she noticed Marcus and Sorrel sitting on the bottom step, arms entwined, oblivious to the world as they kissed.

Her question answered, she went quietly back into her flat.

The Postcard

The postman's left number twenty-seven's gate open again, over the road. She won't be happy. She'll be after him if she sees it. "Can't you see it says clearly *Please shut the gate*," she'll say, and a lot of choice words to follow when she gets into her stride. I suppose she's got a point because the sign's there – I can even see it from my window – but she does go on. The postmen always used to close it, but perhaps they leave it on purpose now, just to wind her up. Or else they don't seem to care as much these days. I think it's since they started letting them wear shorts in summer.

It's like the dustbin men. Time was, they'd lift the dustbin out of my front garden. But now they'll only empty it if it's out on the pavement, ready, on a Monday morning, every other week – or is it Tuesday? I forget. Big green ugly things lined up all along the street. I watch mothers with prams having to squeeze past them, or step out into the road, taking their chance with the traffic. My bin's half in the gateway because I can't move it, but I don't want any of those mothers having an accident because of me. Irina, the home help, makes little deposits of my tied-up carrier bags when she leaves.

The postman's stopped to have a chat with the man with the border terrier. Smart man. Walks the dog the same time every morning and afternoon. Very upright, he is, reminds me of my George the way he walks. He lives a few doors down and passes this way to get to the park.

Two hours, twice a week, Irina comes. She's a good girl, ever so swift. Mind you, I only ask her to do the downstairs now my bed's down here. No point worrying about what you can't see, I tell her, but she pops upstairs about once a month. "Just to keep the cobwebs away," she says. Must be mighty cobwebs because she bangs about like nobody's business, but I don't say anything. She's a good girl.

The best part of her mornings is when she makes me a milky coffee – a *cappuccino*, she calls it – and sits here at the window with me and we have a chat and a piece of the fruit cake she always brings in. I forget where she said her home is but her English has come on in leaps and bounds. Bright girl, too, and she seems to have lots of friends.

"Your china,' she said one morning, after she'd insisted on cleaning all the ornaments even though I don't think it's part of her job description, "your china is worth a lot of money. I have a friend who could sell it for you."

"Too sentimental," I said, though it was kind of her to think of it. "And it's there for my Valerie when I'm gone."

I don't know if Valerie will want it. Last time she came she said she was having the lounge 'de-cluttered' and decorated. "Minimalist," she told me. "That's what I'm after. Clean lines and no stuff anywhere."

Made me chuckle, that did. We must have been 'minimalist' most of our lives. Never had the money years ago to surround ourselves with 'stuff'. It wasn't until the children left home that George started buying me those little bits of china, usually when he'd been a bit lucky on the horses.

Mind you, it's a while since Valerie's had the time to visit, so she might have changed it again by now. Might be back to 'country farmhouse' style – she always likes to keep up with the trends, my Valerie does. No wonder

Kevin's always exhausted. Valerie blames it on having his two sons every other weekend. "Kevin's exhausted", she'll say to me on the phone when the boys have been, so I don't like to make demands on their free weekend, not when she's always got him decorating.

It would be nice to see what they've done to their house.

It's not one of Irina's mornings. But a Meals-on-Wheels girl will be along later with my dinner. I call them all girls, but some of them are getting on a bit now, and one walks with such a limp – arthritic hip, been waiting months for an operation – that I feel quite guilty when I see her squeezing past the bin and hobbling up the path. My favourite's Audrey on Fridays. Somehow she manages to come to me last, so she'll often have a cup of tea with me and a bit of chat, which is nice before the long weekend of soup and sandwiches. Audrey's a bit younger than the others and still has teenagers at home. The things they get up to! Audrey takes it all in her stride, though.

The postman's finished talking to the man with the dog and sauntered on up the street. He'll do up that side and then come back down ours. He doesn't come up my path very often – well, people don't write letters like they used to, do they? I think he might have something for me today, though. Stephen said he'd send me a postcard from Tenerife. A postcard's nice. I can look at it for hours and start to feel that sunshine on my poor old joints. I like a busy harbour scene, where there's lots going on, or the ones where there are several small pictures, so I can imagine what it's like to live or holiday there.

I keep all the old ones in a cardboard box and when the weather's been really bad I go through them all again. They look so bright and cheerful laid out on the table. The places he's been to!

I never get a card from Valerie. Well, they only go on holiday in this country in their caravanette, and she says it's not worth sending cards when she can tell me all about it over the phone. She told me they purposely only got a caravanette so that there wasn't room to take the boys as well. "We'll upgrade," she said, "when the boys are too old to want to come with us." Maybe they'll take me instead. She did mention it once.

My Stephen's a good boy. Always on the phone, wanting me to have this or that. "I'll pay, Mum," he says, "you don't have to worry."

He wanted to pay for me to have those frozen meals delivered, like you see on the adverts, where you just pop them in the microwave. Stephen paid for the microwave, too. But I said, "I like the Meals-on-Wheels, because it's nice having someone walk through the door every day." And I always keep the pudding for my tea.

Last time he rang he mentioned sheltered housing again. "I worry about you in that house all by yourself, Mum. A nice little flat with neighbours and a warden would be ideal."

"I'll think about it," I said. He sent some brochures once, and they did look nice. Hanging baskets and tubs everywhere – I suppose the warden sees to them. But even just thinking about moving is a bit of an ordeal. What would I do with all my things? I'd have to get Valerie over to show me how to become minimalist. She doesn't get the chance to come very often, though, with not being a driver herself, and Kevin's exhaustion.

Stephen said he'd get people in to help me, but I wouldn't want strangers rooting about in all my belongings. I'd rather get Irina to do it and she could probably do with the extra money. Maybe when Stephen's back from his holiday and feeling a bit more rested I'll ask him to come over so we can talk about it some more – perhaps he'll take me to have a look at one of those places. Of course, he'll be dashing about all over once he's home. Drives miles and miles each week with his job, he tells me, especially since he was promoted, so it's a bit much to ask him to come all this way at weekends. "It's only just over an hour on the motorway," Audrey said but I think she's got that wrong. She frowned when

I said, "Oh no, from what Stephen's told me it's a lot further than that," and then she changed the subject. Well brought up girl, she is, wouldn't want to start a debate.

It's funny how all my visitors seem to be women. Maybe they don't let men do Meals-on-Wheels, just in case. It would be nice to see a man now and again, though. The man with the dog always walks back on this side of the road, and if he sees me in the window he gives a smile and a little wave.

A man came from the chapel, once, with one of the women. He might have been the minister, but it's confusing when they don't wear dog collars, isn't it? They said someone could take me to the services if I wanted, they'd fetch me in a car and everything. But there are steps up to the chapel door, and then a nasty turn by the back pews when you get inside, so there'd be all sorts of fuss with the wheelchair I have to use when I'm out and people would be looking. I wouldn't like that.

So I told him, "I'm thinking of converting to Catholic," and I haven't seen him again. One of the women still calls in occasionally – I think she's hoping that I'll convert back. Next time she comes I'll have to mention that I didn't change after all, because I'll be wanting my service at the chapel. At least I won't know about it if they have trouble getting me round that turn.

The postman must be making his way down this side now. I can't see him from here, but number twenty-seven has come out and is shouting across at him. She's got a good pair of lungs on her, because I can hear every word. A shame she uses language like that, though, when the woman from number twenty-nine is taking her little ones to nursery.

They've got loud voices next door, and one of the lads has a set of drums. I sometimes hear them through the wall, if I haven't got the telly on. I don't mind, because it's nice to know there's people around, although I hardly ever see them, but it's very different from when

Mrs. Johnson was there. When I could still get about, she and I used to have little chats over the garden fence, while we both waited. I sometimes wish my waiting had ended, too. Mind you, she'll be turning in her grave at the state of the garden. She always had tidy little borders, but they're all overgrown now, and the lawn's a mess from the boys' football.

Mine would be a mess too, if Stephen hadn't paid for it to be all graveled over. That was a lovely few days when the workmen were here and they were in and out making cups of tea. So cheerful they were. One of them used to sing along to the radio. Lovely voice he had. I told him he should be on the radio himself. "You'd give Tom Jones a run for his money," I said.

Before they packed up he said, "Some of your roof slates are loose, love. I'll have a look for you, sort it out, if you like." I would have let him, but when I told Stephen he said there was nothing wrong with the roof and they were a bunch of cowboys. Cowboys or not, I was sorry when they'd gone.

It's very quiet along the street, now. Everyone's gone about their business, and the postman has just walked by. Stephen will be back in a couple of days, and his postcard still isn't here. He says the post is terrible abroad – some holidays his card doesn't arrive at all. Ah well, maybe tomorrow. Shame there's no second post.

I must have dozed off for a while because the doorbell makes me start. Who can that be? No-one who comes here regularly rings the doorbell, they use that little intercom thing. I hope whoever it is waits until I can hoist myself up and get going with my stick.

It's the man with the little dog, although he's on his own now. He's older than I thought, close up. Still very smart, though. "Sorry to bother you," he says, "but the postman left this at my house by mistake."

He holds out a postcard and I beam. It'll be from my Stephen – I said he's a good boy. I'm eager to read the message and become absorbed in the picture. Last me the rest of the morning, that will, and probably again tomorrow.

I'm just about to take it from him, when, do you know what? I smile up at his face, into his eyes, and, just for a second before he rearranges his features into a polite smile back, I see that look. It's the same look I see when I stare at myself in the mirror. It never used to be there when George was here and the children were still at home.

"I'm just about to have my elevenses," I tell him, "even though it's only just gone ten. Would you like to join me? You must be thirsty after walking your little dog. And I've got some fruit cake in the tin."

He gives me a proper smile this time and that look in his eyes vanishes, replaced by something as warm as any sun in my postcards.

"I don't mind if I do," he says, "thank you very much."

I slide the postcard into my pocket. Somehow it's not so urgent that I read it now. It'll keep till later.

Hearing Loss

The darkness was descending again. It had been hovering around the edges of her consciousness for some time, like wisps of smoke from a woodland campfire. But now it gathered strength, encircling her in black, pressing in on her, as heavy and encumbering as a burqa.

Rob had wondered this morning. "You all right, Anna?" he'd asked, to which she'd simply answered, "I'm fine," and presented her back to him, hunched over the breakfast she didn't want to eat. Reading the newspaper with unfocused eyes. She didn't want to talk about it. There was no point.

Now she somehow had to face a day at work. Put on her bright smile as she listened and advised and tested, and pitied the little mites brought to the clinic; appendages of their young single mothers who gave them outlandish names and spent a large part of the day wheeling them round the indoor shopping centre, wrapped in padded outfits more suitable for a country hike.

She loved them all, though, and told them they were beautiful. Every baby deserved to be told it was beautiful. Many years ago, when she was very small, she'd overheard her mother and an aunt eulogising over what a bonny baby her elder brother had been. "What sort of baby was I?" she'd asked. "Oh, you were a funny little thing," her mother replied. And, deep inside, a funny little thing she'd remained.

So every baby she dealt with was showered with compliments. The truly lovely ones, with big eyes and dimpled cheeks and mouths they had control of from the early months, always smiled and chuckled as if they knew already that they were blessed with the approval of everyone they encountered. So she made even more fuss of the less fortunate, pallid infants with narrow heads and slack drooling mouths, who also seemed already to know their place in the world and were less quick to make eye contact; whilst the infants who appeared in grubby ill-matched clothes, of varying degrees of dampness and aroma, were given extra cuddles, if only to aggravate the clinic assistant, Joan, who wrinkled her nose and looked sourly at their multi-punctured and tattooed mothers.

It made Anna enormously popular with all the parents, especially combined with her knack of making them feel she had all the time in the world for them. A Health Visitor who truly understood what it meant to be a parent.

"Amazing, when she's had no kids of her own," they muttered to each other when she was out of earshot. Within earshot, she was aware of their pitying glances and the unspoken, "What a wonderful mother she'd have been."

In the early years, when the mothers were the same age as her, there'd been many jocular references to when it would be her turn. She'd laughed them off, then, even though she already knew.

"It's much better like this," she'd joked. "I get all the fun of cuddling and playing with babies, and then hand them back for the difficult bits."

As time passed she'd almost convinced herself of this mantra. After all, babies grew into delightful toddlers, with whom she still had contact, but then they turned into difficult children, ugly ducklings often, with second teeth too big for their faces, and obsessions with bodily functions. Even worse, they became mysterious scary teenagers, of whom she had no experience whatsoever, whilst in her world, she had a constant flow of babies and small children of the ages she liked best of all.

She engaged all her senses when handling each baby – breathing in the scent of new skin; marvelling at the silkiness of its hair; revelling in the perfect dimpling of chubby limbs and feet that had never been walked on. So by the end of each day the ache for a child of her own was dulled and, eventually, she hardly ever noticed it. Just occasionally, when visiting some squalid flat that smelled of sex and stale milk bottles, had she to fight the urge to pick up the little scrap brought into the world so casually, and make off with it.

Rob had never minded about her infertility. He appreciated order in his life. He liked to travel and surround himself with fine things. Take impromptu breaks to unusual places, or impulsive evenings out to a new play or restaurant - all the things a young family would have proscribed.

"Happy?" he'd ask her occasionally, when he was enjoying a particular outing.

"Of course," she always replied, because after all none of it was his fault.

There'd been a surge of hope when the first 'test-tube' baby was born, but when Anna meticulously researched the topic she quickly realised the chances of success were slim. And by the time IVF twins and triplets were becoming almost commonplace on her books it was too late for her.

No matter. She continued to 'mother' every baby she met, and a feeling of relief descended as her contemporaries eventually waved their offspring off to university and had to learn how to be just a couple again.

So everything would have been fine except for the dreams.

At first she blamed it on her time of life and demanded hormone therapy from her G.P. But the dreams continued. Dreams where she was pregnant; giving birth;

holding in her arms a baby which she knew was hers because she was filled with such raw love that it was painful and made her wake up in tears. The next time she went, her G.P. blamed it on her time of life and gave her anti-depressants, but they made no difference.

It was a dream last night that was making the darkness descend again. As she drove away from their immaculate cottage, where on winter evenings they sat in front of the log fire like two neutered cats, she wondered, for once, if she could face a day of other people's babies. Last night she'd had a baby girl with dark curling hair and rounded limbs. The baby had tugged on her breast and she'd felt a surge of milk flow from her. She'd awakened suddenly, to a sense of loss and longing so acute that she'd tried unsuccessfully to return to the dream.

Now, as she drove, she experienced a growing urge to drive past the town and simply keep going; on and on to some place where she could escape her present and her past and be someone else. A woman of mystery, free of this senseless longing, free to do and be whatever she wanted. Embark on a love affair perhaps. Sometimes, before a baby arrived in her dreams, there was an episode with an unknown man that produced a passion she'd never felt in reality. Maybe that was what she needed. An encounter where a different sort of rapture would claim her. Her body was still good, unsullied as it was by childbirth.

Impulsively she pulled up outside a bank and withdrew three hundred pounds. Enough to keep her going for a while. Returning to the car she switched off her mobile. The road out of town was long and straight. It beckoned to her, even though she knew where it immediately led. There was still a promise of what might lie beyond.

At first she took little notice of where she was heading, her mind replaying last night's dream as her body squirmed with desire. Her hands could still feel the fragility of that tiny skull as the baby had nestled into her shoulder. The dream seemed more real than anything had ever been in her life.

The grey uniformity of the morning lifted slightly with glimpses of pale February sky visible between moisture-laden clouds. The road carried her through a narrow valley surrounded by undulating hills, with, ahead, a true mountain. She recalled visits here as a child, with an uncle who had carried a rope which he attached to a craggy outcrop and convinced her brother and her that they were really rock climbing.

Suddenly she knew why she had come this way. She had to climb to the very top of the mountain. There she would find the freedom she was seeking and, at the summit, there would be some way of resolving her anguish.

The lower slopes had changed since her childhood; there was a proper car park and signposts indicating the safest route. She was hurrying now, eager for release from her oppression. She disregarded the stouter foot-wear kept in the car boot for when she was visiting outlying farms, and the warmer coat lying alongside. The murky day was mild and she would become too stifled by them as she climbed.

With blazing eyes and the rapturous expression of a mystic she moved purposefully up the mountainside. She should have thought of this before. All the tales through history had approved of solace sought in the mountains. It was where the Greeks went to find their gods, where Moses had been given the Commandments, where Christ has wrestled with the devil. It would be where she would find her epiphany.

She encountered no-one but a few bedraggled sheep, their winter coats tinged with dirt like roadside snow lain too long. There was nothing but the breeze lifting her hair, depositing a fine spray of moisture on her reddened cheeks.

It took longer to reach the summit than she'd thought, the dips and changes in the terrain not visible from the road, but she persevered, ignoring the pain in her feet and the raspiness of her breath as the air grew colder and damper.

Neither, at first, did she notice the mist as it began to swirl around the top of the mountain, just as the blackness had swirled around her mind that morning. Was it only the same morning? She felt so far away physically from all she knew, that time had fractured too. It didn't matter. Nothing mattered. Nourishment, warmth, respite from the increasingly hostile elements - all were irrelevant, unheeded. Here was the release she'd craved.

The mist swooped down to meet her. She lifted her arms to embrace it. It obliterated all indication of any world below. It seeped through her pores to her core, expunging the darkness destroying her.

The ground was still firm beneath her feet and she sensed she was near the top. She kept instinctively moving forward, until the ground levelled out and she knew she was there. For the first time she stood still. All was silent. Only the angel-hair mist continued to circle, eerie wisps of light occasionally oozing through.

Then she heard it, very faintly in the distance. Of course! It was a cry. The baby! Somewhere here she would find the baby.

She turned slowly on the spot. Where exactly was it coming from? She turned again. The swoops of mist confused her. She moved in the direction she thought to be true. Stopped. Listened once more. Yes! The cry, lifting and dropping with the breeze, was nevertheless stronger. Her legs, muscles stretched and torn from the unaccustomed exercise, resisted the instruction to move on, but she persevered, her desperate need driving her. Faster, she must go faster, before the cry stopped and was lost. She heard it again, and knew it to be the baby of last night. She was the baby's mother! Of course she would know the cry!

And now there was a light. Round and yellow, like a torch, shining dimly through the thickening fog. She stretched out her arm towards it but it moved further away. It began to spin slowly, creating a mesmerising vortex, at the centre of which she knew was the baby, waiting for her.

As if numbed she stepped forward, her feet no longer feeling the ground beneath. The light was the answer ... her whole body keened towards it, quivering in anticipation and need. Her lips moved frantically, the words disconnecting as her breath met the air, dredged from Christmasses of long ago when there was still hope in her heart... *In the beginning was the Word ... and the light shone in the darkness... that was the True Light...*

She repeated them over and over, like a Catholic chanting the rosary. There was nothing but the words, and the Light. Beyond it the grey of the mist and beyond that the darkness, gone from her forever. And, nearly upon her now, the cry of the baby... her baby. Her breasts ached in response to the sound, as in the dream.

One final step. Light as air. Her body suffused with joy as the mist raised her up. Suddenly the light rushed towards her, pure white, transforming the droplets of moisture in the air into a million dazzling sequins. She held up her arms as the light engulfed her and the baby's wailing filled her head.

'I'm here!' she cried.

Worried About Jim

Blogspot Housewife 55 : Worried about Jim

September 12th

When I was very small my Mum used to listen to Mrs. Dale's Diary on the radio. From what I recall, Mrs. Dale was a doctor's wife and one of the catchphrases from the programme became 'I'm worried about Jim'.

Well, at the moment I know how she felt. I'm very worried about my Jim. After nearly thirty years together he's decided he's no longer happy with me and has gone off with someone – henceforth to be known as 'The Madam' - who is only a bit older than our eldest. It's completely out of character, the family is devastated, even the cat is moping, and I don't for one minute think he's really going to be happy. Apparently it was my fault because life with me wasn't very exciting, but I think he's gone to the other extreme with The Madam. I mean, he's not as adept at keeping up with modern life as he thinks, while she's still at the age when knowing what's 'in' and what's 'out' helps define who you are. If The Madam starts talking about the 'Arctic Monkeys' he'll think it's a new species David Attenborough has just discovered – no doubt when out and about with the 'Snow Patrol'. I don't think he'll be able to cope. Maybe the children can advise him.

Anyway, on the recommendation of friends, I sought help from a counsellor and she said that sometimes keeping a diary helps to get it all *out of your system. But I know diaries are old-fashioned now. And Jim pointed out – during one of our conversations which quickly escalated into a row – that my being old-fashioned has been one of the problems. Apparently now you 'share' your grievances with your 'friends'. So the younger son, who is very techno-minded, helped me set up this blog.*

It's already feeling very cathartic. Just writing the words 'The Madam' helps me to think of her as someone who resorts to immature tantrums to get her own way. Our daughter used to do that when she was small and would be told she was being a 'little madam', so you'll get the thought process. Jim used to be exasperated with the daughter's tantrums...

Must finish this now – younger son has just called in to see how I am and I want to ask him about a Twitter account. But I'm determined to write this blog every few days – I can feel that it's going to do me far more good than anti-depressants.

Jim has just been round here in a right old state. Apparently younger son told him about my blog, in an effort to reassure him that I was coping well on my own. There are over a dozen entries on it now.

"What on earth compelled you to do this?" Jim asked.

"I thought that was obvious," I told him. "You did. If we hadn't split up I'd have nothing to write about, would I? And you said I needed to keep up with the times, so that's what I'm doing. Anyway you should be pleased. It's better than me calling you to have a rant. You said you didn't like that either."

"But you could have changed my name," he said. "What if people we know read it?"

"Ah, but I've done a bit of a double bluff there," I said. "I thought it wouldn't matter that I kept your proper name, as anyone reading it will assume I've changed it, so they'll think your real name is Tom or something, and won't associate it with you. Especially as I've not used anyone else's names – no identifying marks, as the police might say."

"Well, just to get the record straight, I'm very happy, I don't need advice from my son, and Kirsten's very annoyed that you've called her 'The Madam'."

"Oh dear," I said sweetly, "did she have a tantrum?"

"Of course not!" he answered, but he went a bit red, the way he always did when he was being defensive. "She's not like that at all!"

"Look, I'm dealing with all of this in the best way I can," I told him in the end. "I think I've been very civilised so far, and at least I didn't cut the arms off your suits or anything. Or cut anything else off, so consider yourself lucky. And I don't think either of you need worry, I can't think that my little blog is going to be of interest to anyone else."

Actually, that's not strictly true. I told my friend Valerie about it and when she went to a very boring coffee morning and people were asking her how I was doing, she couldn't help but tell them. I've had quite a few hits so far.

Blogspot Housewife 55 : Travelling the Internet Highway

November 1st

I can't believe I ever managed to exist without the internet! Why didn't I get online sooner?

I've done quite a lot of shopping. I've dropped a dress size since Jim left, which made me think about smartening up my image generally. On reflection, his comments about me being dowdy and behind-the-times were true. So I looked up lots of styles and then had a make-over at the hairdressers – a cut and colour with some interesting highlights, and they also had a manicurist there who went to work while the colour was taking. So then I needed some new clothes to complete the picture, and I must say some of the websites are brilliant. I never realised leggings and floaty tops would be so flattering.

I think Jim's new life is having the opposite effect on him. He's put on weight, which is probably because they eat out more than we used to. A lot of young women don't want to spend much time in the kitchen do they? He was also looking just a little unkempt – his clothes were a bit creased and the collar of his shirt didn't look as if it had seen an iron. I've found an ironing service in the local online directory which I could tell him about.

Or it may be better to email him so that he won't have to get all defensive again. I'll explain to him that I understand that The Madam has a career to think about and can't spend all her time pandering to his needs.

I haven't just used the internet for my personal grooming, though. I looked up so many things, including a list of divorce lawyers. I've narrowed it down to three, so I'm going to take a closer look at their websites and decide an order of preference.

Jim was quite angry when he called round today. He wanted to know why I had begun to look for a lawyer.

"It makes sense to put both our houses in order," I told him. "After all, you and I certainly aren't getting any younger, and we'd be in a right old mess if something happened to either of us and we hadn't sorted out our affairs. We've got the children to think about, and presumably The Mad– I mean, Kirsten – will want to have children one day."

He seemed to blanch a bit when I said that, which made me wonder if he's really thought this whole thing through. I mean, I know The Madam is career-orientated (Jim used that phrase very proudly when he told me about her) but at some point I bet her biological clock will create a deadline she can't ignore. And she excels at meeting deadlines apparently. I looked up her profile on one of those business sites.

Jim decided to change the subject. "This blog nonsense," he said. "I'm sure I wouldn't have said you were dowdy and behind-the-times in such a cold-hearted way."

I didn't reply. Just looked at him sadly until he turned away and blustered about having to get back to The Madam. He mumbled something about liking my new hairstyle as I showed him out.

I watched him as he walked to his car. I hadn't noticed

before that his shoulders slump forward when he walks. It gives him quite a defeated air. Worrying.

Blogspot Housewife 55 : Thank goodness it's only once a year

December 28th

I'd heard that Christmas split between two households could be a bit of a minefield, but I hadn't appreciated just how much of a battle-ground it could become. Now our three are all living away from home I'd thought there wouldn't be too much of a problem. But I'd forgotten the pull of family rituals. They all seemed determined to continue with the time-honoured routines as if to deny there was now a difference. Their innocent expressions when I spoke to each of them about their expectations suggested there had been a certain amount of collusion.

I was very flattered that home still meant so much to them despite the upheaval and the rather desolate air of a house with only one occupant that was evident whenever they visited. The problems really started when they thought their father could be included in all this festive cheer and he also seemed to think that he would be welcomed into the old marital home for at least part of the time. But, apart from the fact that this was not my idea of Christmas heaven, he hadn't factored in that The Madam also had other ideas. Apparently she doesn't 'do' Christmas – although the number of parties and other jollities they attended throughout December showed that she has no objection to the preliminaries. She booked a romantic hideaway in warmer climes for the whole holiday and, when I suggested that they celebrated New Year en famille instead, made it clear that she had no intention of entertaining Jim's offspring in their admittedly cramped but apparently 'delightfully bijou' apartment.

In the end I relented and suggested that Jim joined us for a pseudo-Christmas lunch on the Sunday before he and The Madam were due to fly off. Everyone made an effort to instil jollity into the occasion and it passed off reasonably well until our daughter, probably after one glass of mulled wine too many, burst into tears.

"This is just a sham, isn't it?" she cried, which I couldn't really argue with. "It's never going to be the same again, no matter how much we all pretend it is – I hate it!"

She fled to her bedroom while her two brothers cleared everything away, leaving their parents at the table. Neither of us knew what to say.

Needless to say the actual Christmas Day was a complete let-down and I think we were all relieved when the festive period was over and we could all return to our comforting routines.

But it's all behind us now, and I've made my New Year resolutions, one of which is to completely de-clutter: the house, my wardrobe, my head....

*W*hy are you selling everything on e-bay?"
Jim was on the doorstep, no words of greeting. He was still very tanned from his holiday, but it didn't appear to have relaxed him very much.

"It's to be ready for when this house goes on the market," I told him as soon as I'd drawn him into the kitchen.

"Who said we were selling the house? Your solicitor?"

"I thought it would be an obvious step at some point," I said. "After all, you were the one who said economies would have to be made as you couldn't keep two households on the go. But don't worry, I haven't sold all your books – I've boxed them up ready for you to take."

"But I've nowhere to put them in the apartment," he said.

"Well, I don't need them here anymore. The children bought me an iPad for Christmas, so I shall be downloading all my books. But I'll keep the boxes in one of the bedrooms for now," I said, as he was looking so distraught I was worried about him.

He gave such a big sigh that I felt moved to make him a coffee and offer him his favourite stem ginger biscuits.

"I have to go out soon," I said, "I'm meeting an old school friend I've been in touch with through one of those reunion websites."

I could see that he was wondering if the friend was male or female, but I wasn't going to give him the satisfaction of knowing that it was a woman. He sighed again as he got up to go.

"About this blog," he said. "Did you have to put so many details about Christmas on it? I think two of the women at the office have been reading it."

"Ah, I was going to tell you about that. I've been offered a job, of sorts – the local paper has been in touch. The editor has been following the blog," (actually I think Valerie may have put him on to it) "and wants me to write a regular column – *Life of a Divorcee,* that sort of thing."

"But we're *not* divorced!" It's a while since I'd heard his voice raised so loud.

"No, not yet – but what would you prefer? *Life of a woman dumped for a younger model?*"

"I'd prefer," he said, through gritted teeth now, "that you didn't write anything at all – no column, no blog, no twits or tweets or whatever they're called. I really don't understand you anymore."

"But Jim," I reminded him innocently, "you were the one who wanted me to change. And you know, you were right. I've embraced the modern age and I feel so rejuvenated. I tell you what – in my next blog I'll make sure I mention my gratitude."

Blogspot Housewife 55 : A proposition

February 10th

I've had a message from an old school friend via the reunion website, which I thought I should share as it surprised me so much.

Dear Sandy,
I don't know if you remember me, but I was the boy who fell in love with you in the upper sixth. We had a wonderful summer together

after our exams and I thought we would stay together forever. But the years pass, things change. I've changed and I've been looking back on my life and I've realised that the things I valued the most I've let slip through my fingers. I've read your profile and realise that you're different too, but I bet underneath you are the same sweet girl I fell in love with. You say that you are single again, as am I – could we meet and recall old times and see whether there is anything from all those years ago that we could re-kindle?

Yours hopefully,
Danny

It took me right back. To when love was exciting and precious and full of hope. I've never forgotten that time, and it must have taken a lot of courage to get in touch, so I've said yes! We're meeting on Valentine's evening. I'm very nervous, it's years since I've been romanced! Watch this space.

The lounge bar was very busy but I got there early and managed to find a cosy corner. He was early too and looked every bit as nervous as I felt.

"The last I heard, you were in a relationship," I said.

"It was a mistake," he said. "We went on holiday and I knew with every passing minute that this was not where I wanted to be. So I finished it. In the New Year."

He looked directly at me then for the first time since he'd arrived.

"I've been a fool, Sandy," he said. "An old fool, straight out of the classic stories. I couldn't see what I had until it was too late and I know if I don't ask you if there is any chance of us being together again I'm going to regret it for the rest of my life."

Despite the years that have passed, his was still the same face I'd fallen in love with so long ago. And now the love and the longing were back in his eyes, just like those magical years when he became 'Danny' to my 'Sandy', because Grease was our favourite film, and *You're The One That I Want* was our song.

"Oh, Jim," I said, "I've been so worried about you."

I've learned a lot since Jim left me. I've learned all these new ways to communicate, but I've also discovered that no matter how many Facebook friends you have, or how many times a day you tweet, or how many people read your blog, there is no substitute for the man you love being there by your side, even when no words are spoken.

It will be hard to build up the trust again, but we have to try. Jim is still the one that I want, so there's plenty of reason to work at it. So for now I'll say farewell to my blog and the internet superhighway – except, perhaps, for the shopping. The rest will just be between the two of us.

Voice of Romance

*A*nd now, taking us up to the nine o' clock news, we have a 'rave from the grave' – the Beatles and 'Get Back'. And I'll be back with you bright and early tomorrow morning. Until then, it's good-bye from Laurie Hardman and the Breakfast team."

The velvety-smooth voice of the local radio presenter faded as the music began. With a sigh Sarah swung deftly into her usual parking place and switched off the car radio and the engine. Time to finish daydreaming and concentrate on earning a living.

She stood for a moment and looked with distaste at the back of Dalton's, the main store of a large hardware chain where she worked. The pay might be good, but shut away in the office upstairs dealing with accounts and invoices frequently relating to sanitary ware and drainpipes was hardly in keeping with the fantasies she indulged in about the life she'd really like to lead.

The gleaming black bonnet of the car belonging to her boss nosed its way into the car park, which made her quickly scuttle inside the building. Mr. Taylor was kindness itself, but he did like to see her at her desk opening the mail when he walked into the office.

By mid-morning she had dealt efficiently with all outstanding work and Mr. Taylor was ensconced in his office with a sales rep. Time for a break. She poured herself a coffee and extracted a paperback novel from her handbag.

Deeply engrossed in the tortuous adventures of a luckless but beautiful heroine, she jumped out of her seat when the office door was suddenly flung open. "Oh! I wish you wouldn't do that!" she exclaimed, mopping up coffee from her desk with a tissue.

"Sorry. Didn't mean to startle you." The smiling young man perched amiably on the edge of the desk. John was the store manager and had worked hard over the past few months supervising a large extension being added to the ground floor of the store which was to sell all sorts of gardening items and patio furniture.

He accepted the cup of coffee that Sarah offered him and then leaned confidingly towards her. "Guess who is going to make the official opening for us? Laurie Hardman!"

Sarah nearly spilled her coffee for the second time that morning. "Laurie Hardman?" she repeated in incredulous tones. "Coming here?"

John's smile widened into a grin. "Thought you'd be pleased. I've been arranging it for ages but didn't want to tell you until it was definite. He's coming a week on Friday."

Sarah and John had become friends soon after she began work at Dalton's. John, intrigued by the long-legged girl who had taken over from the ancient Miss Betts, had found numerous excuses to visit her office and had helped her out of many difficult situations when the complicated system she had inherited from Miss Betts had led her to send bills instead of receipts, or reminders to accounts already settled. Sometimes they met after work for a drink, or spent a Saturday afternoon going for long bracing walks in the country-side. Sarah considered John to be a good friend, but certainly not the man of her dreams. His fresh freckled face turned red in the sun and looked decidedly peaky in winter and he still had the gangly limbs of a teenager, despite the fact that he was well into his twenties.

Laurie Hardman was the man who had occupied

many of Sarah's daydreaming moments. His voice on the radio, when he was flirting outrageously with the weather girl, never failed to thrill her, and his pictures on the internet certainly matched the sexiness of his voice.

"Of course, you might be thoroughly disappointed," John was saying now. "Those publicity shots will all have been air-brushed. They might not even be him at all – like those photos you see of people on dating sites who don't look anything like that in real life. He might really turn out to be fat and balding with a wart on his nose, and that's why he's chosen to work in radio. Your mornings might never be the same again!"

In a moment of rashness, Sarah had confessed to John her unashamedly fanciful nature and the dreams she nurtured of being swept off her feet. And that Laurie Hardman would certainly fit the bill for her.

"Don't be silly!" she said stoutly. "No-one could sound like he does and not have the looks to match." She leaned towards John as he finished his coffee. "And since when have you been looking at internet dating sites?" she asked, which made him blush to the roots of his hair – something Laurie Hardman would never do of course. She took pity on John, so quickly added, "Anyway, I think it's wonderful – you couldn't have chosen better."

He leaned forward too, so that their heads were nearly touching. "And I did it all for love of you!" he exclaimed in dramatic tones.

She chuckled and gave him a little push so that he had to stand up. "Get away with you! I'm the great romantic around here. Leave me in peace to think about what I can wear on the big day!"

John left, an exaggeratedly injured expression on his face, and she turned her attention to entering invoices on her computer, although it was hard to concentrate. How could she get Laurie Hardman to notice her amongst the rest of the staff?

*I*n the event she had more opportunity than she had expected. A few days later Mr. Taylor called her into his office. "Ah, Sarah. I have a big favour to ask you, I'm afraid. The directors want to make sure this Laurie Hardman is given a bit of celebrity treatment when he's here, and have arranged for the canteen caterers to put on a buffet lunch in the boardroom. The trouble is, they need – well – someone to oversee the arrangements, and act as a hostess, for want of a better word, so I said that I would ask you. Bit of a cheek, I know, but you don't have to agree if you don't want to do it."

Not want to do it! She tried to make her voice sound cool, but her heart was beating wildly. "Well, I'll ignore the sexist implications of the request for the good of the firm," she said, "seeing as I know how much they have invested in this new department. I'll be pleased to help out."

The week leading up to the opening flew past. Sarah experimented with her long hair in a different style each day, producing a variety of comments from John, not all of them flattering.

"I don't know why you're bothering – old Wart-Nose is probably short-sighted anyway – and, of course, he might just bring his wife along."

"If you ever listened to his programme," Sarah replied, in a tone that she hoped sounded withering, "you would know that he is footloose and fancy-free – just like me!"

John was prevented, by a call from one of his team, from making a caustic rejoinder as to the possible reasons for Laurie Hardman being available. He there-fore contented himself with pulling a face at her before leaving, which made Sarah giggle and push him out of the door.

*F*riday, The Big Day, arrived. Dressed discreetly but attractively in a navy-blue dress which emphasised her slim figure, Sarah joined the rest of the employees in the new department. Soon after eleven he arrived – and was everything Sarah had dreamed about. Tall and dark, his face lightly tanned and creasing regularly into a beguiling smile, he oozed suave sophistication. Every bit as good as his photos.

Sarah listened to the voice she knew so well confidently going through the usual rituals of such events, and was happy to stand well back in the crowd. Her chance to meet him properly would come later.

"I bet he spends every day on the sunbed to get a tan like that – and he's far too old for you," came a voice in her ear.

Sarah didn't take her eyes off Laurie.

"You're just disappointed that he hasn't got a wart on his nose," she chuckled, and went off to make sure everything was ready in the boardroom.

For the next hour she was extremely busy, handing round plates of food to the assembled group and ensuring that there was a steady flow of wine and soft drinks. All the time she was aware of Laurie Hardman's presence and his liquid voice charming all around him.

Eventually one of the directors gave a little speech to thank Mr. Hardman for officiating. "And I would also like to thank Sarah, who has worked very hard to make sure that we've all enjoyed this lunch!"

There was a ripple of applause, and Sarah found Laurie Hardman's interested gaze upon her. As the guests began to talk amongst themselves again, he moved towards her.

"Sarah! One of my favourite names!"

They talked for several minutes, his attention never wavering from her face, making her feel special.

"I'd like to add my thanks for a wonderful lunch – and so attractively served," he said finally, his voice low, almost murmuring. "Perhaps I could show my appreciation further – how about dinner? Tonight? If you're not already spoken for, of course."

"No! I mean... Yes!... I mean..." Sarah took a deep breath to compose herself. "No, I'm not 'spoken for, and yes, I would love to have dinner with you."

His deep-set brown eyes bore into hers, so that she

could understand how old-fashioned heroines swooned. "Good. Pop your address down for me and I'll pick you up at eight o'clock."

He produced, of all things, a little black book, but the page he offered Sarah was an empty one. She wrote her address and phone number down and handed the book back. He gave her a little smile of complicity and a "see you later" before his attention was claimed by one of the directors.

John had been standing at the other side of the room, watching them. "Well?" he asked. "Satisfied now you've spoken to your hero?"

"Better than that!" she replied, her eyes shining. "He's asked me out to dinner tonight."

She hurried off to supervise the clearing away, and failed to see the misery in John's normally cheerful face.

Laurie collected her promptly at eight, and took her to a quiet, expensively elegant restaurant, with stern, intimidating waiters, where he appeared to be well known. Sarah was overcome with nerves and an aware-ness of her inexperienced youth, but Laurie seemed not to notice her reserve.

"Of course, local radio is only a start," he told her. "I'm planning to move into national radio very soon, and then hopefully some television work – just need that lucky break, that's all!"

"And I'm sure you'll get it!" Sarah breathed, think-ing how handsome he looked in his dark suit and crisp white shirt, which flattered his tan. It was easy to imagine being held in his arms and leaning her head against his broad shoulders.

Afterwards he took her to a nightclub that was filled with people who all seemed to be his friends, judging by the way he greeted them. They were all successful thirty- and forty-somethings who laughed a lot and made witty jokes at each other's expense, but rarely got up to dance. Sarah was happy to watch them, aware that she was entering a world of which she knew nothing.

It was the early hours before he drove her home. "I

hope I haven't worn you out," he said, although she noticed tired circles beginning to contrast with his tan.

At the door he kissed her, carefully, briefly, on the lips. "Do you like jazz?" he asked.

"Love it," Sarah replied, crossing her fingers at the lie.

"Good," he said, in the same masterful manner he had used when inviting her out earlier. "Come to Gordino's with me tomorrow night – best jazz in town. I'll pick you up again about eight."

Saturday was spent in a frenzy of anticipation combined with remembering how he looked and how he had spoken to her the previous evening, and a frantic phone call to one of her friends to ask what one wore to a jazz club. She had finally chosen wide-legged black trousers with a white top in soft crepe and had let her newly-washed fair hair swing loose on her shoulders, just caught on one side with a simple slide.

His eyes roved over her approvingly as he escorted her to his car. "You look stunning!" he told her. He had dressed casually himself in chinos and a T-shirt, but still looked immaculately groomed.

The jazz club was dark and very smoky, and the music loud and discordant to Sarah's unaccustomed ears. Laurie sat holding her hand and tapping his feet to what, as far as she was concerned, was a largely inaccessible beat. Nevertheless she nodded and smiled when he asked her if she was enjoying herself. She was loath to admit that she preferred the modern pop music that Laurie played on his show. When the music stopped they ate supper, Laurie answering all her eager questions as to where he lived and what his other interests were.

"And what about you, Sarah? What do you like doing when you're not fighting off the attention of dozens of amorous men?"

She smiled at the compliment. "Oh, I like... tennis... and reading..." She sought desperately for something interesting. She thought of her long walks with John. "And I love being in the country..." She decided not to tell him about the hours she spent tending the plants which overflowed the small balcony outside her flat.

He pulled a face. "I'm afraid I don't seem to have the time for much reading, and I'm strictly a townie – although I do like to go and unwind in the countryside now and again – as long as the hotel has a spot of night-life and a well-stocked bar!"

She didn't like to ask him about his fresh-air suntan for fear of John's comments about the sunbed being true.

He kissed her again outside her flat, more linger-ingly this time, until Sarah was just about to melt in his arms and succumb to inviting him in, when he stopped abruptly and consulted his watch.

"Oh, Lord!" he groaned. "Is that the time? I've got to be up early tomorrow to record an interview for the show!" He looked about to take his leave when he stopped and turned back to her. He stroked her shining hair with his hand. "Beautiful girl. I'll 'phone you just as soon as I can."

By Monday morning, with work beckoning, it seemed to Sarah that the weekend had almost been a dream. She had spent most of Sunday agonising over whether he would in fact ring her. She switched on the radio and heard Laurie's voice again and felt reassured. She was just picking up her handbag when she heard him say, "And this one is just for the beautiful Sarah!"

She swept into the office as if on air, eager to see John and tell him all about Laurie. But John didn't come into her office all morning, and he wasn't in the staff canteen at lunch-time.

Mid-afternoon he popped his head around her office door. "How was the weekend?" he asked, but then nodded and said, "Good!" when she had got no further than 'wonderful'. "Do you fancy a drink tonight?"

"Oh, John, I can't, I'm afraid." She couldn't go out.

Laurie might 'phone and she wouldn't be there to take the call.

"It doesn't matter," he said. "Must dash. Very busy."

By Wednesday Sarah was thoroughly despondent, convinced that Laurie wouldn't ring. By Thursday evening she was ecstatic because he had. On Friday and Saturday they wined and dined and met lots more of Laurie's friends until she felt quite dizzy with the hectic pace of a completely different social life.

The weeks gradually fell into a pattern. Sarah would spend most evenings at home, waiting for Laurie to call or text and then burn the candle with him at weekends. Saturdays were spent beautifying herself or buying new clothes for the evening ahead, and Sundays were spent recovering. Sometimes there would be parties, sometimes a show, often a club – and nearly always with many other glamorous people.

One or twice she succumbed to temptation and telephoned him on a lonely weekday evening, eager to hear his voice speak just to her, but it always went to voicemail and he didn't ring back.

But despite their continuing romance, there was an elusive quality about Laurie. Sarah felt that there was an inner core to his character that she still didn't know. Fed on the brooding heroes of Jane Austen and the Brontës, she told herself that this enigmatic trait was a necessary factor for a truly romantic man and that all that was needed on her part was time and patience, and the opportunity would present itself when he would open his heart to her and declare his undying passion. Perhaps all that was needed was a little more opportunity to be alone together, but he hadn't seemed very keen the one time she suggested a quiet evening in, so she had never repeated it.

One night, however, he told her that the following week he had been invited to a weekend house-party in the country, and he wanted Sarah to go with him. "There are going to be some interesting people there, including a producer who seems rather keen on my work, so it should be an exciting weekend – and you, my pet, will stun them all with your charms!"

Sarah was ecstatic. She had to admit that she missed her long walks with John, and it was the time of year that she loved. Roses were in their first full bloom, the country air would be heavy with the smell of honeysuckle, and the weather was beautifully warm, promising a long hot summer ahead. Best of all, no matter how many other people were staying, she was sure there would be some opportunity for them to be alone.

She spent the first part of the week wrapped in daydreams of Laurie declaring undying love for her as twilight fell. But by Wednesday her vision began to blur and her throat to ache and she realised with horror that she was coming down with the summer 'flu that had already decimated a large part of the workforce at Dalton's. She spent all of Thursday in bed, her head throbbing too much even to listen to Laurie's soothing tones on the radio.

By the evening she knew she had to call him and warn him that she might not be well enough for the weekend. This time he answered the 'phone.

"Poor darling!" he sympathised when, in muffled tones, she bemoaned her fate. "What rotten luck! Listen, sweetheart, you know I would love to pop over to see how you are, but I daren't risk the voice."

"Of course," she responded, quite certain that she didn't want him to see her looking so dreadful, anyway.

"Now you take good care of yourself," he went on, "and I'll call you again before I set off for Sussex tomorrow evening."

On Friday she switched the radio on and tried to listen. Perhaps he would give a get-well message over the air to cheer her. But she kept dozing off, and missed most of the programme. She consoled herself with the knowledge that he had promised to call later, and tried to ignore the aching in her limbs. She spent the evening huddled in an armchair next to the 'phone, willing it to ring, but it remained silent. Too dispirited and too ill even to cry, she dragged herself off to bed.

Next morning she was determined to resurrect her optimistic spirit. There would be an excellent reason why Laurie hadn't called. More than likely she would receive a large bouquet of roses today as an apology; he had said he would make it up to her when she had said how disappointed she was to miss the house party.

When the doorbell rang she dragged herself out of bed. She knew she had been right about the flowers! Sure enough, when she opened the door there was a large bunch of flowers, but the hand holding them was John's. His eyes widened with concern. "Hi! I thought you could do with a bit of cheering up – you look dreadful – have you seen the doctor?"

"Oh John!" she cried, the sight of his friendly face proving too much for her. And with a grace that would have done justice to the best Victorian heroine she swooned into his arms.

The next thing she knew was waking in her bed, with the comforting aroma of soup emanating from the kitchen. As she tried to remember what had happened, John appeared and placed a mug beside her.

"Hot lemon and glycerine – made to my old grand-mother's recipe! Drink it up while it's hot."

"You shouldn't have gone to so much bother!" she exclaimed as she struggled to sit up.

He grinned. "It's out of a packet, really – but I'm sure my grandmother could have made it! The soup's out of a packet, too, but you ought to have something. Do you think you could try some?"

She sipped the lemon drink, grateful for its soothing warmth, and decided, her throbbing head notwithstanding, that perhaps she could try the soup too.

"Has... er... Laurie been in touch?" he asked her casually as he stood over her while she ate and drank.

"He's away... for the weekend... he couldn't miss it, unfortunately – it was all tied up with his job.

"Anyway," she went on, catching sight of her blotchy

face and red nose in the dressing table mirror as she struggled to control her trembling lips, "What would he think, seeing me in this state!"

"Whereas those of us who truly love you see your beauty all the time!" he bantered lightly.

She managed a small smile. "It's all right. You don't need to make jokes to cheer me up. You've done that already."

His face suddenly straightened. "Perhaps I wasn't joking," he said seriously, before carrying her tray out to the kitchen.

John arrived again on Sunday and prepared a light lunch for her, and sandwiches that she could eat later for supper.

"I'm beginning to feel better now," she told him as they sat together by the French windows overlooking the patio. "You shouldn't have gone to so much trouble for me – but I really do appreciate it." She was surprised to find her eyes filling with tears of gratitude. Silly how weak this 'flu made you.

He stood up and kissed the top of her head. "That's what friends are for," he said lightly. "I'll call in tomorrow morning on my way to work and see how you are."

She spent the evening alternately agonising over how she had neglected her friendship with John over recent months, and hoping that Laurie would call on his return from the country house, until, neither hope nor guilt resolved, she fell into a fitful sleep.

He arrived promptly next morning to find her drawn but definitely over the worse and sitting by the radio. "I'm so much improved," she told him, "mostly because of your help, I'm sure."

"I'm glad," he told her, and there was no mistaking the warmth in his voice – a warmth that suddenly thrilled her in a way she hadn't experienced before. "I must admit you had me worried for a while – especially on –"

He broke off as Laurie's voice came over the airwaves. "And this one is just for the beautiful Kimberley! What a girl! What a weekend!"

John leaned over and switched off the radio. For a moment they stared at each other in silence, and then the easy tears which had threatened yesterday could no longer be controlled. In a second he had enfolded her in his arms.

When at last her sobbing stopped she nestled her head against his shoulder. It seemed absurdly right. She knew now that Laurie Hardman's intentions had never been serious; all Laurie wanted was a pretty girl on his arm while he pursued his ambitions. It had been her own fanciful hopes that had read more into the situation than there really was.

John stroked her hair. "I always said you should never trust a man with a fake tan."

She made a sound somewhere between a hiccup and a laugh. "I've been a complete fool," she said. "I really thought Laurie Hardman was going to fall wildly in love with me – and all the time you were in the background, being a real friend when I needed one."

"And if you let me," he told her, holding her close, and sounding extremely masterful, "I'll be the most romantic man you've ever met."

She moved in his arms, a smile lighting up her red-rimmed eyes. She no longer saw the freckles and the gangly limbs. Just a caring face, concerned only for her.

"I do believe you will!" she said.

Close To You

*H*ave you ever loved someone so much that just thinking about them makes your insides scrunch into a pain that moves up through your body and lodges in your throat, so that you can't answer properly if somebody else speaks to you?

I don't mean lust. Lust is the feeling you get when the girl in the newsagent's at home leans over the counter to give you your change and you get a flash of her ample breasts jostling each other for space in her push-up bra. Or when you watch the college netball team and the tall, slender girls stretch up to shoot at goal, their toned thighs exposed below their short skirts, as if to deliberately entice. You can feel lust at any time, or most of the time.

But love... where the other person fills not just your body and mind but your soul... where your senses are so heightened that you just know when she's entered a crowded room... where your peripheral vision becomes so acute that you can plot her progress without even turning away from the person you're listening to... where all you crave is to spend a few more moments basking in the warmth of her regard... that's something else.

I'd never felt like that until Lindsey. I'd only had one girlfriend – Alice, who was in the same youth group as me. She would look at me with doe eyes and cling with a smothering, limpet-like devotion. And we never got much further than hand-holding and a bit of a grope on disco nights when the lights were low.

Lindsey arrived in the middle of our first year at college, sweeping into the Junior Common Room with an energy that made everyone else feel dull and sluggish. You could tell from the way we all sat up straighter, or stopped slouching by the bar, or just looked expectantly at this new person, that we hoped by a strange osmosis we would become infused with her golden glow, if only she would notice us.

She'd been living in the States but, her father being a diplomat, she was now back in Britain and had transferred her studies. Her low, melodic voice held no transatlantic twang, but the American influence was apparent in other ways. You could see it in the artfully sun-kissed streaks in her long, blonde hair. And in the perfect dentistry, which was probably the result of many adolescent months of mouth metal, and in the light brown sheen of her skin, when we were all suffering from a dearth of sunshine and too much winter comfort food.

"Hi!" she said to the room in general, with a self-assurance which probably stemmed from only ever receiving the world's approbation from the moment she learned to smile. "Sorry to be a nuisance, but could anyone help me – I don't have a clue where I'm supposed to be going!"

Of course, while I was still thinking about it, three or four of the more agile and confident lads were there, ready to pick up the assortment of bags she'd dumped on the floor, and show her where the girls' accommodation was. I hung back, never having believed that I could actually be much help to anyone anyway, and watched as the little party trooped through to the doors at the far end of the room, the lads already bathed in the light that seemed to surround her and which intensified as she smiled her thanks.

I spoke to her later, though, when a group of us were playing brag in the bar and she came in with Leanne who, it transpired, was in the room next to her and had volunteered to show her round.

"… and these are the piss-artists," Leanne told her as they approached our table. "This is Andy, who only turns up to lectures when he's threatened with being chucked out, and this is Dave, who gives the *best* parties, as long as someone helps him with his assignments. And this is Ollie, who thinks he can sing…"

"… and I'm Kennie," I said, holding out my hand, before Leanne got to stick a label on me.

"Hi Kennie," she answered, her eyes looking steadily into mine as she took my hand. "Good to meet you."

I searched her face for a moment, before letting go of her hand, to try to gauge any deeper emotion in her expression, but her keen sapphire eyes showed just the same interest and regard as she had for the others.

Of course, within days the lads were falling over themselves to be the first to get her to go out with them, and our little group shifted ourselves with almost as much energy as the rest to win her approval, even though we were the jokers and the idlers.

Except for me. I wasn't really the same as the rest of my friends, although I affected an equally casual nonchalance towards life's challenges. But deep down I was a worker, always had been. I didn't have the security that some of the others had – an insouciant charm which would always get them through, or an innate ability that even extreme laziness couldn't extinguish. I knew that to get anywhere in this world I was going to have to try harder than most of those around me. So much of my time was spent in the library, working on my laptop. The others still accepted me, though, because I was easy-going and laughed at their jokes and didn't make them feel guilty about being work shy.

It stood me in good stead with Lindsey, because she had a strong work ethic, partly inherited from her family background and partly from the more diligent American student attitude. So she'd regularly be in the library too, and as often as not I could manoeuvre to be in the place next to her. Or, even better, opposite her, so that I could watch her covertly as she studied.

"Hi Kennie," she'd say, with the bright smile and good humour which rarely faltered, "what is it today?" And we would compare notes about our work for a few minutes before settling down to what we had to do. She was studying politics, so I made a habit of getting to the library early and scouring the broadsheets so that I could make erudite comments about current world affairs.

Naturally there were a couple of girls who were jealous of this new queen bee around whom the drones swarmed, and there were a few sarcastic comments from some of the lads, who, knowing they were right out of her league, suggested that she was probably frigid or gay.

But none of this lasted, because Lindsey was impossible to dislike. She was the same with everyone – generous, happy, funny, bonding with the girls and willing to muck about with the boys. You hear about people having the ability to light up a room with their presence, but this was the first time I had seen someone who could do that. I'm a bit of a sucker for those old Seventies songs, and now Karen Carpenter was constantly singing in my head, *"Why do birds suddenly appear..."*

After a few weeks of Lindsey-watching I could see that she was attracted to Ollie, who, when he made the effort, was witty and clever, which, combined with dark good looks, had already enabled him to notch up more conquests than anyone else. And, of course, he happened to be my closest friend.

Now it was two heads, one blonde, one dark, bent over their work in the library, Ollie having discovered that he had a leaning towards learning after all. With exquisite pain I watched the two of them and could have told you, from the changes in their body language and intimate glances, when they started sleeping together.

And I so, so, wanted it to be me on whom she bestowed

that privilege. In the privacy of my room I ranted at the gods who'd seen fit to pass me by when good looks and wit were given out. I dreamt of holding her in my arms, and seeing a look of tenderness in her eyes turn rapidly to passion.

It would have been better if I'd withdrawn gracefully at this point and not tortured myself with being so frequently in their presence. But I relied on Ollie's friendship as much as I needed a daily draught of Lindsey's golden presence.

"Don't hurt her," I begged him, when I could see that she was beginning to need him more than he needed her. But Ollie just shrugged. She was beautiful and desirable, but then there were so many girls... so little time.

By now I knew many things about her. For instance, I knew that when she went out in our damp English weather her fringe developed a kink which she unconsciously tried to smooth with her fingers as she talked. I could tell from the slight change in the texture of her skin and a hint of shadow beneath her eyes when she had been working too hard or spending too many late nights in Ollie's room. I knew the causes she was passionate about, and that sometimes there was a slight stutter in her voice when she was pleading her case. I knew that she twiddled with the earring in her left ear when she was concentrating on writing and that the jokes I sent her by text when lectures were boring made her smile.

And I knew when Ollie began to get bored with monogamy and I saw the incredible iridescence of her eyes become slightly clouded. After she'd sent two rapid texts which remained unanswered and then slumped back in her chair in the library with a hint of defeat in her shoulders, I leaned across and squeezed her hand.

"He's not worth it, you know. You can do much, much better."

She tried to give me the old smile then, and almost succeeded. Then she stopped, moved round the table and sat beside me.

"You are so sweet," she murmured in my ear. Then, with the merest whisper of her lips on my cheek, "I'm so glad we're mates."

"Mates!" I wanted to shout at her. *"Sweet!* I don't want to be *sweet!* Or just *mates!"*

I wanted to be her hero! I wanted her supple limbs to be entwined with mine, to feel her skin against my skin. I wanted her to tell me that she longed for my athletic body, that she thrilled at the sound of my voice, that I entertained her, made her laugh, made her feel the most wonderful woman in the world! Something – anything. But not *sweet.*

But I didn't tell her any of this. Because I'd always known that she was never going to be for me. My destiny, once I'd finished college, was the Alices of this world. An earnest, caring girl, who would be there with a patient face just short of martyrdom whenever I needed her. Someone over whom the social workers could coo and privately agree that she was the answer to a huge problem once they'd sorted out a home for us. And then they could have meetings to decide whether it was physically possible or socially desirable for such a flawed being to reproduce, without anyone voicing the question everyone really wanted to ask, *"Do you think he can actually do it?"*

I didn't say any of this to Lindsey either. Trying very hard to speak without a trace of bitterness, because that's the one thing people can't stand, to see that you're bitter about the hand life has dealt you, I simply said, "Yes, we'll always be mates."

And, holding tightly onto the feel of that brush of her lips because it would have to last me a very long time, I turned my electric wheelchair around and set off down the corridor.

Faint Hearts

*M*ost people would visualise a park bench to be beside a path in a big open space, maybe overlooking a pond, with carefully manicured flowerbeds nearby. Mothers with small children stopping to throw bread to overfed ducks, that sort of thing.

Well, this one wasn't like that. This park perched above the town on a hillock shaped like a honeypot, with the path meandering untidily around it. It was a bit of trek to reach the bench at the top, but it was worth it for the view of the town spread out below.

Frank liked this bench. He sat on it most mornings in fine weather, watching – once he'd got his breath back from the climb – all the people down below getting on with their lives.

"It does you good," he said to Violet when he was explaining where he went each morning for his 'constitutional'. "It's like when you look at the sky full of stars and realise how insignificant you really are in the overall scheme of things. Puts your problems in proportion."

"Problems?" said Violet. "What problems have you got?"

"Well, none at the moment," he admitted. "But when I have, the bench is where I sort them out."

He had a problem on this particular day, though, and the problem was Violet. Most people called her Vi, but not Frank. "You must have been named for the colour of your eyes," he told her not long after they met. "They're like Elizabeth Taylor's."

"Ooh, go on with you, "she said, but he could tell she was pleased. So he always used her full name after that.

That was a few weeks after he'd moved into the retirement complex and was getting to know his new neighbours. Violet was the one who introduced him to everyone and got him involved in all the social things. He probably wouldn't have bothered otherwise. All the years he'd spent on his own had left him finding it difficult to join in.

"Of course, they're a nosey lot round here," Violet told him. "So don't tell them anything you don't want the whole world to know."

Well, that wouldn't be a problem. He'd never been the best talker, and all the time on his own had pared his conversational skills to a minimum. He found himself telling Violet lots of things, though. Like how long he'd been a widower and how he'd floundered once retirement loomed and he wasn't sure what to do with the years ahead. That's when he'd started sitting on the bench.

And Violet told him all about her large family and introduced him to most of them. She told him how her husband had died when her children were still quite young and how she'd managed to bring them up without a man under her feet.

She was still very organised, so that they'd fallen into quite a routine together. Each morning after his 'constitutional' they met for coffee, either in each other's flat or, if the day was particularly nice, they'd wander over to the community centre and have a cake as well. Then later there might be a social event Vi had convinced him they should attend, or they'd watch a TV programme together.

Violet would listen while Frank harrumphed over newspaper items he disagreed with, and he would listen when she had some family matter on her mind. He liked the way she was so independent and strong. Not like some women he'd encountered during his lonely years who seemed to expect a declaration of intent after more than one cup of tea together. To his relief, Violet didn't go in for all that romantic stuff.

"There's too much of that sort of thing on the telly," she'd said more than once. "It's better left to the imagination."

It was one of the reasons they got on so well. They both knew where they stood and liked it that way.

So why, this morning, when she stepped through his front door and into his kitchen, with her usual, "Halloo – only me," and he'd seen her, framed in the doorway, those beautiful violet eyes enhancing her special smile, had he been filled with a desire to step forward, take her in his arms, and kiss her?

The urge had shocked him so much he'd stopped in his tracks.

"Are you all right?" Violet had asked. "You've gone all pale. Here – you sit down and I'll make the coffee. You've walked too far up that bloomin' hill I expect, and it's already hot this morning."

He'd been so unresponsive to her usual chatter that she'd left him to rest and said she'd call in later to see how he was. But he didn't need to rest, he needed to think, which was why he'd walked back up the hill this afternoon, to the bench where, somehow, he was able to think more clearly.

He was in love with Violet, he knew that now. What an old fool he was! Falling in love at his age, and with a woman who clearly valued his friendship but needed nothing more. The gossipers would have a field day with that bit of news if it ever got out.

He was going to have to give himself a stern talking-to, to get his feelings in check and be able to continue with their friendship the way it had been.

He knew he couldn't talk to Violet about it. He wouldn't have the words and everything would be spoilt.

*A*lex trudged wearily up the hill. It wasn't the same without Yasmin by his side. They did this walk together every day after school, so they could sit on the bench, holding hands, and look down on the people below going about their lives, while they planned how their own lives were going to go.

But there was someone already sitting on their bench. An old man. That had never happened before, they'd always had it to themselves. Not that it matters now, Alex thought. Who cares who's on the bench if I'm here on my own?

He sat at the far end, hunched into his misery, thinking of Yasmin and the happy, innocent hours they'd spent together here.

Frank wondered if he should make his way back down the hill when the young lad plonked himself down on the bench. Perhaps he was meeting someone here. But a few sidelong glances showed Frank that the lad didn't seem to be here to socialise. His head was sunk in the collar of his jacket and his hands thrust deep in his pockets, his whole body language sending out a message of pain that Frank recognised from long ago.

When the sniffing started, becoming more and more audible and prolonged, Frank couldn't stand it. "I don't know about you," he said, "but the breeze up here makes my eyes water sometimes. Here – could you use one of these?"

He thrust a pack of paper handkerchiefs towards the boy. Vi had popped them into his jacket pocket a while back. "Got them on special offer," she'd said. "You might need them for rescuing damsels in distress."

Well, it wasn't a damsel sitting next to him, but there seemed to be quite a bit of distress going on.

After a moment's hesitation, Alex took a handkerchief from the pack, before handing it back to Frank with a gruff, "Thanks."

"Why don't you keep them," Frank said, "in case you need another one."

Alex thanked him again and stuffed them in his

pocket. He had a pleasant face, Frank thought, even when it looked a bit blotchy. The sort of lad Frank would have liked for a son – or a grandson, come to that. He wanted to ask him if he was all right, but wasn't sure what to say.

Violet would have known – she could strike up a conversation in an empty room, and she had several grandsons. This could be one of hers, clearly upset about something – she would be proud of him if he went back and told her that he'd helped.

The thought of Violet left him all of a dither again.

"It's a grand view up here, isn't it? " he said, as much to distract himself as the lad. "I come up here every day – but usually in the mornings."

There was no reply, so Frank thought again. "I've come up here now, though, because I've got something on my mind. It's a good place for thinking things through."

That was it. The sum total of what he felt he could say. It was silly to have even started a conversation.

There was a long silence before the boy spoke. "We come up here every day, too – at this time, after school. Just to sit and talk."

We? Oh dear. Frank would much rather he'd said he was in trouble at home, or at school. But that clearly wasn't the problem. He'd have to say something else now. "But not today?"

Alex shook his head. "Or any other day from now on. Her father found out. Said we'd been going together behind his back and that Yasmin's too young for boyfriends and that I would 'bring dishonour to her'." He kicked out at a small pebble at his feet. "But it wasn't like that. We only ever held hands and talked. Now we can't see each other at all."

"That's hard," Frank said. "Maybe when she's older…"

Alex shook his head. "We leave school next year. We'd planned to go to college together, then we'd get married. But now her father has decided he doesn't like me he'll probably make sure she goes somewhere else."

"But her father doesn't know you've made these plans?"

The boy shook his head again. "We knew he might be difficult, so we were waiting for the right time." His head sank down onto his chest, as he kicked futilely at the same pebble. "But there never will be a right time now. He doesn't want us to be together."

Frank thought about how Violet dealt with her grandsons when difficulties in their young lives threatened to overwhelm them. *Straight talking,* she called it. Even though she peppered her speech with euphemisms and adages that sometimes made them perplexed, they always got the message in the end. He could try it, he supposed. He cleared his throat and prepared to make his voice strong.

"Well, it's no good sitting here feeling sorry for yourself, is it?" This produced a hostile glare, but he soldiered on. "You need to go and see him."

"What?"

"Well, it seems pretty obvious to me," Frank said, warming to his theme a little as at least the lad hadn't got up and walked away. "He's put his foot down because he thinks you've been messing about with his daughter and –"

"We weren't messing about!" Indignation made the boy sit up straight and Frank could see the passion in his eyes. "We love each other – and I respect her. I wouldn't do anything to hurt her or 'dishonour' her."

"So tell him that. Ask him if you could meet Yasmin under whatever conditions he demands, until he trusts you."

"What, like having to sit with her family and stuff?"

"If that's what they want – yes. If you love her as much as you say you do, then you'll do whatever it takes." An adage that Violet would be proud of came into his mind. "After all, *faint heart never won fair lady.*"

Alex slumped back on the bench, deep in thought. Frank said no more. Instead he concentrated on watching the people far down below.

After a few minutes Alex spoke. "You think that would really work?"

"Well, it's better than doing nothing, isn't it? And he can only say 'no', but at least you'll know what you're up against."

Alex stood up. "Maybe... maybe I'll go round to her house tonight, when her father's home."

Frank smiled at him. "Good for you. And good luck."

He watched as the lad made his way down the zig-zag path. Perhaps he'd come up here again one afternoon in a few weeks and see whether they were together. He would have to tell Violet he'd found the words.

Violet. What was he to do? For a moment he envied Alex his troublesome youth. He had his whole life ahead of him to love and be loved. But he, Frank, was at the age when those things were considered over. When romantic declarations could, at best, be laughed at or, at worst, be pitied or viewed as vaguely disgusting.

He was so absorbed in these thoughts that at first he didn't recognise the figure weaving its way up the path.

"Trust you to be right at the top. I'm all out of puff." Violet leaned on the back of the bench to get her breath back. "I saw you leave – thought you'd be here. Which means there's something on your mind. Which got me worried."

Her eyes, those beautiful violet eyes, when he looked up at her, were certainly full of concern. But more than that. Could it be...? What had he said earlier about *faint hearts*? He and Violet didn't have as many years ahead of them as that lad and his Yasmin, so there was even more need for straight talking. And she could only say 'no'.

He cleared his throat and prepared to make his voice strong.

"Sit down, Violet," he said, taking hold of her hand. "There's something I want to tell you."

Maybe

The social worker's just left. She clearly couldn't wait to go. And I can't blame her, really. I'm just another name on her caseload – a square-peg troubled teenager that she has to fit into the round hole of a foster family as quickly as she can. Do the job, tick the boxes, contact all those other people who are laughingly called my 'corporate parents'. Which means I don't have any real parents – none that deserve the title, anyway.

I'm standing in the kitchen, with my defiant face on and my worldly goods in bags around my feet. The new carer is smiling at me with her eyes, but she's biting her lip. *Nervous – is she nervous?* She doesn't look like my other foster carers. She's wearing Doc Martens for a start. Bright green. That's different. Usually I get put with the older, experienced ones in cardigans 'cos I'm classed as 'hard to handle'. Maybe I should call the social worker back and tell her she's got the wrong place, but her car's already shot off down the road.

Perhaps it's my Goth make-up making her nervous. I wait for the introductory chat, where she'll tell me confidently that everything will be 'fine'. That I won't feel a complete loser when I turn up at a new school with not quite the right uniform and not quite the right gym stuff, and not quite the right attitude to fit in properly because there's too many things I don't want to talk about. They always try to tell me everything will be fine. How do they know how it feels?

But she doesn't do any of that. She just says, "I like being called Liz, by the way."

"Shall I show you your room, so you can put your things away?" she asks.

"Do I have to go to bed, then?"

She shakes her head. "No, of course not – you need to settle in a bit first.'

"Is it just me here?"

"No. Jamie, my son, is in the other room watching telly. He isn't being rude, he just thought he'd say hello later, rather than have us both gawping at you."

Interesting. She knows I don't like being stared at. Last time the whole family was lined up so I felt like one of those royal people on a special visit when they say something polite to each person. So I ended up saying nothing, and I could feel their disappointment.

I follow her up the stairs. The room's not bad, very plain and smells of new paint.

"You can sort it out however you want. Put your own stuff around, put posters up or whatever – make it your own."

She follows my glance to the bags. 'Bags for life' it says on the sides, which is about right as all my life is inside them.

"I haven't got any posters," I tell her. "Don't usually stay long enough 'cos I don't usually fit in."

I raise my eyes, fix them on hers so that she understands. "Then I get moved somewhere else."

On the bed there's a pile of clothes.

"It's school uniform," Liz says, not flinching at my stare. "When they told me you were coming I asked how tall you were and then popped out to get a few things. There's two sizes there – I can take back whatever doesn't fit. Oh – and I didn't get trainers, 'cos I didn't know your shoe size, but maybe you've got some already?"

New. It's all new. I've never had new uniform before –

it's always been bits and pieces from the ones before me, or what the social worker's brought... Tell a lie. I had a new school pullover once, when I was about eight. My old one had gone missing, so Mum bought me a new one, as a birthday present. Can you imagine? She'd completely lost it with me, telling me I was useless, so that was all I deserved for my birthday. When I went into school next day I told the other kids I'd been given a pony, but of course they didn't believe me.

I pick up a navy sweatshirt, breathe in its newness. It feels really soft.

"Is it all right?" Liz asks.

I want to tell her it's lovely. I know I should say thank you, but the words won't come out. I even want to make a joke and tell her it's not my birthday, but she won't get it, and if I try to explain I know I might end up crying, and that's what you never, ever do. You never let them see that they've got to you, 'cos it might all disappear again. So I just nod and say, "It's fine."

Back downstairs we go into the lounge where a boy with long legs is sprawled on the sofa with a small white dog lying across his knees. The boy looks too old to be her son. She must have been really young when she had him. The dog jumps down to greet me with unbounded enthusiasm, but the boy stays where he is while Liz tells me, "That's Jamie."

He looks up briefly and says, "All right?" before switching his gaze back to the television. I make a fuss of the dog so I don't have to answer him. Liz is hovering by the door as if she doesn't know what to do either. In the end I ask her, "So, what are the rules?"

"Rules?"

"Yeah – house rules. I usually get told them at the beginning."

Then tomorrow I'll be given a whole set of other rules by the teachers – a 'designated teacher' if the social worker's done her stuff, which means all the other kids'll know I'm in care. Only we're not kids in care any more, we're 'looked after children', which is a bit of joke, isn't it? I mean, if my Mum had looked after me in the first place I wouldn't be here, would I?

After the teachers I'll try to take in all the unwritten rules so's I don't look too stupid. Like, which way to carry my bag, what are the cool things to like, who are the kids to speak to and which ones to avoid, and what are the key words to use so I sound the same as everyone else so I don't get picked on. Just the thought of it is so daunting that I feel the urge to cry again. I give a big, unattractive sniff instead.

Liz's looking a bit uncertain, which suggests to me that she's not much good at this fostering lark. How's she going to cope when my Mum tries to get in touch and my world goes black and confusing and I start to lash out?

"No smoking inside or outside the house – so you may as well get rid of your stash now – no drinking, no drugs, and come home at the time you say you will." Jamie's still watching the telly while he reels these off, but then he sits up and grins across at Liz. "And no swearing – unless you're having a rant about something and can't stop yourself, but then you have to apologise when you calm down."

Liz grins back. "What he's trying to tell you is that it might be me having the rant – but I promise I always apologise! And now he's blackened my character, I'm going to put the kettle on."

Does the social worker know about this, I wonder? I'm usually put with foster parents who never ever get rattled, but this one's admitting she shouts and swears. Maybe she's not had any training. Maybe she's all they had left.

The dog's back on the sofa, but Jamie hasn't gone back to watching the telly. I feel like I ought to say something but can't think what.

"How did you know I've got a stash?" I ask in the end.

He shrugs. "If I was moving in with complete strangers I'd need a fag to keep me going. Won't work here, though."

"No-one's ever stopped me before."

"You haven't lived with my Mum before."

We'll see about that, I decide, stomping through into the kitchen. Might as well get the first wind-up over with, then she'll know what she's dealing with.

"I smoke," I say. "A lot."

She nods. "Anything else?"

"Um... I... um..."

"Because you see," she goes on while I'm still wondering what else to admit to, "when it was me in care, I used to do everything. Smashed a room up once, ran away a few times, got caught shoplifting by the police. I hated not having a proper home so I made sure everyone got so fed up with me they never gave me the one thing I wanted."

She's read my file, must have done. How would she know all that stuff otherwise? There's this pain in my chest, pushing at me, making me breathe funny. A kaleidoscope of memories fills my head. Bad, all bad. All the stuff I try to lock away till it erupts like a volcano and spills over when the blackness comes. No-one's ever commented on what's happened before. Every time it's been 'a fresh start', and I've seen the zeal in their eyes as they take up the challenge of Molly.

"You're making it up," I tell her, my voice jagged because she's looking at me like she can see right inside me. No hesitating now. She rolls up her sleeve and points to long thin scars on her arms. "That's where I used to cut myself. One of the stupidest things I did. But I couldn't deal with the pain any other way."

I don't know what to say.

"You can ask Jamie about his story as well, if you like – it's pretty impressive," she goes on. "We adopted him a few years ago."

She grimaces. "I say 'we', but his Dad left. I'm still not too good on the adult relationships bit. But me and Jamie, we get along fine."

Misfits. They've put me with a pair of misfits. I've been with all sorts before, big families, small families, but never a pair like this. And they've never been this upfront. Doesn't she know she's supposed to dance round me really carefully in case I take off?

But she's looking me in the eye again, and I can't look away.

"We know, Molly. *We know.*"

And perhaps she does. Perhaps she knows I never mean to do all those things, but I get sucked into them somehow. Sometimes fitting in with the troublemakers is at least better than not fitting in at all. Sometimes it's only the troublemakers who'll tolerate me.

"Would you like that cuppa now?" she asks.

"Can I take it upstairs?" I've got a bit of thinking to do.

"Of course. Whatever you like. It's your room now." She smiles at me.

My room. Maybe this time it will be.

Maybe she'll understand when I drop my bombshell. Maybe she'll help me keep the baby. Maybe she'll know this is the only thing I've had that's mine.

I give a tight smile back. It's a start.

Miss MacGregor

"Kiri! I'm home!"

Miss MacGregor pushed the front door closed behind her and looked round expectantly for a sleek tabby cat to come and writhe and twist around her legs, purring a rapturous welcome.

But nothing happened.

Surprised, she put her purchases on the kitchen table and opened the back door. Although there was a cat flap in the bottom of the door, Kiri rarely left the house when Miss MacGregor was absent, apparently preferring to wait until her mistress was safely home.

Afternoon sunshine streamed into the house. Perhaps Kiri had been unable to resist its lure today. Miss MacGregor strolled around the garden, calling the cat's name encouragingly, but still she didn't appear

Absently dead-heading a few late summer roses as she went, Miss MacGregor returned to the house and unwrapped her shopping. She would put Kiri's favourite liver on to cook and leave the back door open. That would soon entice her back.

As she worked, she tried to stop herself from worrying. "Kiri's far too sensible a cat to get into any sort of trouble," she said aloud, in the way she did when the tabby was sat on the windowsill and seemed to heed every word. Nevertheless she continued to scan the garden from time to time for a sight of the companion who had wrought significant changes to her life over the last year or so.

Retirement from a long career as a midwife had coincided with the death of her mother and, suddenly, she had been on her own, each day stretching ahead, waiting to be filled – by what?

She had hoped, once she had recovered from the immediate loss, that Mother's passing would give her the freedom she had sometimes yearned for during the long months of being her mother's carer. But once that freedom arrived, with the option to do whatever she wanted, she could barely remember what it was she'd been yearning for.

It would have been easier if she had had someone to make plans with, who would reassure her that she wasn't going to make a fool of herself. But she had never been very good at establishing the sort of easy rapport with people that leads to friendship. Instead she had hidden behind professional formality; first as simply 'Nurse', and then, as she climbed the midwifery ladder, she had been 'Miss MacGregor' to everyone she encountered, so that now she rarely heard anyone use her Christian name.

There was Edna, of course. But their friendship had arisen out of nothing more than their mutual predicament of having to care for elderly parents, and, although Miss MacGregor's mother was now dead, Edna's difficult father was still very much alive. But Miss MacGregor no longer wanted to hear about caring for an irascible relative, and Edna showed little enthusiasm for Miss MacGregor's eulogies about her rapidly growing cat. So it was becoming increasingly obvious that Edna was growing as bored with their weekly encounters as she herself was.

Nobody could have been more surprised than Miss MacGregor at her acquisition of a kitten: it was the first 'impulse buy' she had ever made. She had wandered into town one early autumn Saturday afternoon when the wistful breezes stripping the trees gave her a melancholy feeling. She was aware that she was becoming shrouded in aloneness, which ultimately wouldn't be healthy.

"Perhaps I need a pet," she thought. "That's what other people seem to do when they are living on their own."

She headed for the market where she knew there was a pet stall, with the vague idea of buying a budgerigar, not because she particularly liked birds but, having thought of getting a pet for company, a bird seemed to be the easiest to manage.

She probably wouldn't have noticed the kitten, the last of a kindle, if it hadn't been alone in a cage directly in line with her field of vision. And she would probably still have ignored it if it hadn't woken at that moment, stretched delicately and then stared at her with eyes that looked huge in its tiny face. It gave a small squeaking sound which seemed to speak of its abandonment.

Looking round to see that no-one was watching her, she began to murmur to it, the kitten immediately tilting its head to one side in response to her voice so appealingly that, before she knew it, she was asking the stallholder how much he wanted for it.

"Twenty-five pounds," he said immediately. Experienced at sizing up the gullibility of his customers he had asked for five pounds more than he had intended to for this runt of the litter.

"Lovely markings she's got," he went on. "Cost you twice that much in a big pet shop."

As he spoke he opened the cage and handed the kitten to Miss MacGregor, who, upon feeling the kitten nestling up to her trustingly, was immediately lost.

She carried the kitten home snuggled up inside the top of her coat, one hand protectively holding it while the other hand grappled with bags containing bedding, cat litter and food which the man insisted she needed.

By the end of that day she was experiencing feelings of tenderness and love for the tiny animal that completely overwhelmed her. During all her years as a midwife she had never felt like this over any of the babies she had brought into the world. A warm glow of satisfaction at a job well done, yes, and pleasure in a mother's delight, yet always aware that her involvement was purely professional. But this soft fluffy little creature had only her to depend on for its survival and its need dominated her days for the next few weeks.

She rather self-consciously called the kitten 'Kiri' after her favourite opera singer, and watched with pride as she grew and became increasingly independent. The acquisition of Kiri not only provided Miss MacGregor with a *raison d'etre,* but also widened her social contacts. Visits to the vet for vaccinations, and grave discussions with the pet stallholder about flea collars and fresh food versus canned broke the routine of her ordered existence.

Only Edna disapproved, and sniffed disdainfully whenever the cat came near her.

"That's your mother's chair!" she gasped as Kiri leaped onto its soft cushions and nonchalantly took possession of it. "And whatever would your poor mother think about the arms!" Which, it had to be said, had suffered greatly from daily use by Kiri for sharpening her claws.

But Miss MacGregor no longer cared about the chair, or Edna's obvious conviction that she was becoming a bit soft in the head since her mother's demise. Kiri was bridging the awful gulf that had opened when Mother had died, and, apart from Christmas time when Miss Macgregor became painfully aware that she was alone in the world, she was happier than she had ever been and far less aware of her solitary status.

She had developed a tentative friendship with the lady in the library. Miss MacGregor, thorough as ever, had gone to find books on caring for cats and had plopped a large selection down on the desk.

"Ah! A fellow enthusiast!" The librarian was a plump comfortable woman, and had smiled widely at her whilst efficiently stamping the books. "What breed of cat do you have?"

"I believe she's a tabby," Miss Macgregor replied, trying hard to rid her voice of its cold formal sound, produced by shyness but which many of her old colleagues had misread as frostiness.

But the librarian appeared not to notice, and happily eulogised about cats in general, and the two she owned in particular. "People say a dog is man's best friend, but I don't think you can beat a cat curled up on your lap for company."

Many cheerful conversations had then ensued, not just about cats, but about other shared interests and pastimes whenever Miss Macgregor visited the library. She had been pondering lately as to whether she should invite Mrs. Sibley to tea, but it was difficult to shake off the natural reserve of a lifetime, and Mrs. Sibley, despite being a widow, seemed to lead a very busy life with a large brood of grandchildren to fuss over.

Miss MacGregor chopped up the cooked liver and put it in Kiri's bowl. "Kiri! Come on Kiri!" she called through the open doorway, rattling the dish. But still she didn't appear.

By nightfall Miss MacGregor was seriously worried. Kiri had never stayed out so long before, except for a few wanderings in the spring, but since then she had stayed in the house and the garden almost exclusively, and had even filled out quite a lot as she'd grown up.

Unable to settle, Miss MacGregor wandered around the quiet empty house, its solitude pressing in upon her without her feline friend for company. Suddenly a faint noise made her stop in her tracks. She stood very still and listened – yes, there it was again; a thin, almost supernatural cat sound, not quite a miaow, not quite a yelp, coming from her bedroom.

She quickly entered the room, trying to locate the sound, when suddenly the valance on her bed twitched. Swiftly she whisked the valance up, got down on her knees to peer into the gloom underneath the bed, and there was Kiri, lying on her side, her eyes large and pitiful in the dim light.

"Oh, my poor Kiri!" cried Miss MacGregor, stroking her head as the convulsion subsided. "Whatever is the matter?"

Thoughts of poison ran through her mind. The poor creature was obviously very ill and in great pain. She tried to remember details of feline ailments that she had conscientiously read about, but all she could think of was that her cat might be dying.

She tried to lift her out from under the bed, so that she could see if there were any signs of injury, but just as she slid her hands underneath her body, the cat gave another shuddering heave. She pushed the bed away instead, and then gasped in amazement at what was before her – a perfectly formed, tiny kitten.

"Oh Kiri!" she gasped, incredulously. "Oh Kiri, you clever, clever, girl."

The cat struggled to raise herself and began to lick the sticky little body, but after a few moments her abdomen began to contract again, and she gave a small yowl of discomfort as she returned to her labour. Before Miss MacGregor's awed gaze, she disgorged two more kittens in swift succession; a tabby, and a ginger one. Miss Macgregor continued to watch, entranced, as Kiri, as soon as the births were complete, competently set about disposing of the afterbirths, rigorously cleaned her new family, who were already making tiny squeaking sounds, and then lay down to let them discover the warm satisfaction of suckling.

Miss MacGregor sat on the floor next to the cats, absolutely stunned. She hadn't for one moment considered that her cat might be pregnant – and she a trained midwife! The vet had tried to persuade her to have Kiri neutered but Miss MacGregor had resisted as she hadn't wanted to put her pet through an operation, and anyway, to her mind, Kiri wasn't that sort of cat.

She looked tenderly at the tiny kittens and was pleased that their mother had decided to do what a cat must obviously do. Untoward events had not loomed large in her life and now she felt as dazed and excited as if she herself had played a greater part than that of mere onlooker.

"What am I supposed to do with you all now?" she wondered aloud, to which Kiri gave an unconcerned answering miaow. She couldn't leave them all there on the floor for the night, but she wasn't sure how or where to move them. She vaguely recalled that if you handled baby rabbits the mother would eat them, but she wasn't sure whether it was the same for cats.

Beset by these fresh anxieties, she tried to think of what she would do if she were a midwife attending an unexpected confinement. "Rest, quiet and nourishment," she recited firmly, more to reassure herself than her cat. She quietly left the room and returned with Kiri's bed, which she lined with a worn flannelette sheet and one of her old cardigans; for tonight she would keep Kiri and her babies in her room, and find out in the morning whether it was safe to move them.

She put the bed in a corner of the room and then wondered how to get the kittens into it. But Kiri solved the problem for her, by leaving the now sleeping kittens while she investigated the arrangement, and, having decided upon its suitability, she delicately lifted each kitten in her mouth and deposited it on the soft bedding while Miss MacGregor watched in breathless admiration.

By the time Miss MacGregor had provided a litter tray, and food and drink for Kiri, and then attempted to clean the bedroom carpet where the confinement had taken place, the elation was beginning to wear off. She wished desperately that she had someone to share the amazing events of the evening with. Edna would not be interested, and there was no point calling the vet when Kiri had managed everything so beautifully. Then she thought of Mrs. Sibley. Would she mind being contacted out of the blue?

She knew Mrs. Sibley's address and forced herself to

find her number in the book, then stood in front of the telephone, hesitating, but eventually lifted the receiver.

"My dear! How nice to hear from you," said Mrs. Sibley straight away, as if they spoke on the telephone regularly, instantly dispelling Miss MacGregor's doubts, so that it was easy to spill out the excitement of what had occurred.

"How wonderful!" Mrs. Sibley exclaimed when she had finished. "Sounds as if you've done all the right things," which made Miss MacGregor glow.

"I don't have to be at the library until midday tomorrow," Mrs. Sibley continued. "Perhaps I could pop in on my way? I love to see newborn kittens."

"Why not come earlier and have morning coffee with me?" Miss Macgregor was surprised at how easily the invitation tripped off her tongue. "And please... call me Mavis."

Mavis Macgregor lay in bed later that night listening to the contented shufflings and snufflings coming from Kiri's corner. She would be busy for weeks looking after Kiri's new family until it was time to find homes for the kittens. And tomorrow she would get up early to bake some scones before Janet Sibley arrived.

For the first time in many years, the future stretched out blissfully in front of her.

If Dreams Were Wishes

hey say that supermarket shopping is often the way to find romance – some of them have those special 'singles' shopping events, don't they? But it was the last thing I expected as I stacked my trolley with the family pack of loo paper and multibuy baked beans. In fact, I was miles away as usual, wondering if this summer would actually see me stretched out on some exotic beach. A new, miraculously slimmer me, reminiscent of my younger days. I often spend my time doing this. It's the only way to get through the weekly mundane ritual.

So when I felt a tap on my shoulder and this dark chocolate voice saying, "Hi – it's Gemma, isn't it?" it took me a moment to get back to reality. Then I wondered if I had, because I turned round to come face to face with Jason Bingley – *the* Jason Bingley, of college days, whom practically every girl in my year had fallen for at some time or another. My first thought was one of thanks that I'd just had all that work done on my hair. My second thought was that he still had all of his.

"Jason Bingley?" I said. "What are you doing here?"

"Same as you – stocking up on a few essentials." He indicated the basket in his hand which contained a jar of olives and some bits and pieces from the deli counter. "I've just moved into one of the new riverside apartments."

We exchanged pleasantries for a few minutes, while I marvelled at his still white teeth and athletic figure, simultaneously moving around so that I wasn't directly below the harsh shop lights.

"Look – this is such an unexpected pleasure," he said eventually, after we'd moved away from a dedicated shopper whose path we were blocking, "do you fancy having a coffee and catching up on old times?"

He nodded towards the cafeteria which mercifully was quiet at this time of day. I hadn't reached the frozen foods yet so I could spare half an hour. He was looking at me with that same slightly quizzical, slightly wolfish George Clooney smile that used to make me melt all those years ago. It was having a similar effect now.

"That would be lovely," I said, and then wished my answer had been a bit more sophisticated. As we walked along the aisle I picked up a pack of wildly expensive fresh coffee from the organic shelf, along with a couple of jars of something I didn't actually recognise and looked faintly like pickled body parts, but they hid the baked beans well.

"So, Jason Bingley," I said, after I'd chosen Earl Grey tea, even though I don't like it very much, and nobly resisted my usual custard doughnut. (We always called him *Jason Bingley* in that breathy italicised way that girls have when they're infatuated, and always used both names so as not to confuse him with the other Jason on our course, who definitely didn't stand up to comparison.) "So, Jason Bingley, why an apartment back in this town?"

"I'm opening a new business next week – the estate agent's in the middle of town. The market is booming at the moment. And what about you," he went on, "did you ever become an air hostess?"

"Um... no... I kept my feet firmly on the ground, in fact. Got married and had three children instead. They're all teenagers now, of course. Only one left at home."

I quickly steered the conversation back to him,

unwilling to dwell on the fact that we'd known each other so many years ago that the eldest 'teenager' is already in his last year at university. Or that marriage and children had come along so quickly after college that the best I'd managed was three days a week as a secretary since the youngest started school.

He told me lots about himself, though, including the fact that he was divorced some years ago, and we exchanged snippets about other friends we'd kept up with.

The time flew by until I had to tell him that it was time for me to go.

"I hope you settle in well – the Riverside development looks beautiful," I said.

Thankfully he took the hint.

"Would you like to come and see my place – while I've got a few days free?"

I tried to sound nonchalant as I agreed, but my heart was racing. We settled on the next afternoon and I finished my shopping and went home in an even more dreamlike state than usual.

Home to the chaotic household that a sixteen-year-old daughter can create all by herself and to a husband, Dave, who was now back home before me and was already putting the kettle on.

"I'll unload the car for you," he said. "You've probably bought lots of stuff, with the boys both coming home this weekend.'

He did look quizzically at the jars of body parts, but I quickly said, "The boys like them," and stuffed them to the back of the cupboard, while he smiled fondly at the way I indulge our kids.

Now it's at this point that you're probably expecting me to start having second thoughts about meeting the handsome debonair Jason again when I've obviously got such a good man at home who loves me dearly. But I'm sorry to say I didn't. You see, I'd been absolutely besotted by Jason at college, and he'd broken my heart. I couldn't let this second – no, let's be realistic, this *final* opportunity to make up for all the past just go by without another thought.

And anyway, I was only going to have a look at his apartment, and the Riverside development had been the talk of the town for ages... And we were old friends, what's wrong with old friends getting together again? It didn't have to mean anything... and...

I must admit to having a Bridget Jones moment the next day, when I struggled with which type of underwear to put on. But that was only because the becoming little dress I'd chosen was really becoming a bit tight and I had to decide if I could spend a couple of hours breathing very carefully while consoling myself that underneath I looked very feminine indeed, because obviously only I would know that.

Jason opened the door almost as soon as I'd rung the bell, and kissed me fleetingly on the cheek while holding both my hands in his. He led me into the centre of a large open-plan living space.

"I thought we should celebrate meeting up like this again," he said, handing me a glass of chilled wine. "I assume you still like white?"

Actually, tastes change, and I much prefer red, but I took the glass with a murmur of appreciation, aware that his eyes were on me intently and they were full of admiration. It had been a long time since I'd felt so desirable.

Luckily, the apartment was a good diversion every time he stood so close to me that I could feel his breath on my collar and my heart started jumping about again, and it really was no effort to breathe shallowly, which helped with the silhouette.

"This is amazing," I said, my gaze taking in the pale wood and smoked glass furnishings and minimalist lines, all dominated by a huge window looking out over the river. A large, slim plasma screen was on the opposite wall, there was surround-sound music, and the kitchen had lots of chrome and dark granite and state-of-the art gadgets. Everything looked very expensive.

And very plain, of course, and uncluttered, but then he'd only just moved in.

"It'll be lovely once you put your own stamp on it with a few bits and pieces," I told him.

"Hmm," he said, looking at me a little oddly. Then, "Let me show you the bedrooms."

Dangerous ground, here, of course, but he was nothing but a gentleman, and the ultra-modern en-suite was such a delight that I was genuinely enthusiastic.

But I knew that at some point he would kiss me. We both knew it. Let's be honest, it was what we were both here for, if my reading of our body chemistry was correct.

He took me in his arms when we were back in the living room and had just toasted to future prosperity. He held me tightly as I closed my eyes and went back to being eighteen again. And as his lips covered mine I would like to say that, in an explosion of ecstasy, it was the most wonderful, thrilling, sexiest kiss I had every experienced. But it wasn't.

Oh, it was very slick, practised, almost professional I'd say, but as disappointing as that moment when you bite into a strawberry cream only to find you've chosen the ginger surprise.

But it was when he nuzzled the side of my neck and murmured, "Oh Gemma, I can't believe we've found each other again," that I knew it was over before it had begun – for the second time in my life – and I had to be honest.

I pulled away from him slightly and looked him squarely in the face. That handsome, chiselled face with the startlingly blue eyes which I saw now held nothing behind their blueness.

"I'm sorry," I said. "I can't do this. You see, I'm not Gemma. I'm Jane, the girl you went out with, fleetingly, before Gemma. The girl you didn't take out again because Gemma had caught your eye."

He didn't answer me straight away, but I realised that the look of shock on his face was the first genuine expression I had seen on it so far.

"Why did you let me think that you were Gemma?" he asked eventually.

"Because I was flattered that you thought I looked like her – she was always the girl I wanted to be," I said slowly.

"Gemma did become an air hostess, by the way," I went on, mainly to fill the awkward silence. "And she's still doing European flights and living in Surrey with her third husband. Never got over her wanderlust, I suppose, whereas I – well, I thought I had some sort of wanderlust too, but I haven't."

"I'm sorry," I said again as I gathered up my things and beat a hasty retreat in what can only be described as a less than dignified manner.

Before I got into my car I looked up at the new apartment block. It was very cleverly designed to blend in with the ancient buildings surrounding it. A beautiful exterior hiding an interior with not much in it at all. Just like Jason Bingley, I suppose. But the building was attractive enough to make you want to see inside every time you walked past, and, if you were feeling a little bit down on your luck, to imagine that living there would give you everything you'd dreamed about.

That first time we'd gone out, Jason had never even kissed me once. And I'd spent the last twenty-plus years imagining what it would have been like if only he'd given us more of a chance. But now I know that those were dreams as unreal as the apartment building.

So I was going home to Dave, whose hair started to recede about the same time as I started to go grey. But somehow his craggy features have grown into the changing contours of his hairline, in the same way as my features have responded to all the changes of style and colour.

In the summer we'll probably both lie on a beach somewhere not too exotic and not mind that neither of us is as streamlined as some of the people around us. But when he leans across to kiss me, as he often does on holiday, his lips will find mine and tell me all I need to know about being loved, and I'll love him back.

We'll be adding to all our memories, which I know now are much better than dreams.

Somebody to Love

I'm waiting for Liz to pick us up. She said she had a bit of shopping to do first, but that's fine. For now it's nice just sitting here in my hospital room and taking it all in. It's still a bit of shock to think this little bundle in my arms is mine. My baby. My responsibility. After all the fuss I made about keeping him, there's no going back now. Not that I'd want to. I didn't know it would feel like this. I'd talked to him already, of course, whenever he was making his presence felt. And even when he wasn't – during the nights when I couldn't sleep, I'd lie there stroking my swollen belly and whispering promises. Mainly about making sure he'd get a better deal than I had.

But I still didn't realise how it would feel. And now, when he's barely a day old, the love I already have for him is almost savage in its intensity. Which makes me wonder – did my Mum ever feel this for me? In a way I hope she didn't – 'cos then I'd have to think that somehow it wore off, and I never want what I feel for my baby to wear off.

I kept the pregnancy quiet for as long as I could, in case all the people who have a say in my life tried to persuade me to end it. But Liz, my most recent foster carer, guessed. I should have known she would. From the first day I was placed with her – me, the trouble-some teenager that no-one else could cope with – it was like she knew everything about me without being told. And while everyone else pretended not to be shocked, I knew she *really* wasn't.

She came into my room one morning when I was getting ready for school and trying to get my trousers to do up. Although she'd knocked like she always did, I wasn't quick enough to turn away from her. Perhaps by now I didn't want to.

"I think it's time we talked about this, don't you?" she said, sitting down on the bed so that I knew she wouldn't budge even if I tried to use being late for school as an excuse to avoid the conversation.

"Who's we?" I asked. "You and the social workers and everyone else who thinks they know what's best for me?"

I could hear the hardness in my voice and hated myself for slipping back into the scowling, sneering person I'd escaped from during the weeks that I'd been with Liz, but it's hard not to when I feel threatened. Liz ignored my tone, though. She's expert at doing that. "I just thought you and me for now," she said. "We could talk about you seeing a doctor and a midwife, those sorts of things – and then decide together how we tell all the other people."

"I'm not getting rid of it," I told her, "I don't care what any of them say."

"I think you'll make a good mother," she said. "Probably better than I was at first – you told me when you got here that you smoked a lot, but you haven't had one, I know. That shows you've been thinking of the baby all along."

"And you're not going to send me away?" I asked. It had been my biggest fear since I'd begun to settle in here, and another reason for keeping quiet for so long.

"Send you away?" she said. "When I've not had a baby in the house to cuddle for ages? I'd much rather you stayed here – if it's what you want, too."

So I didn't go to school that day. Liz sent a message with Jamie, her son, to say I was ill. I wasn't ill, though, all the way through. The whole pregnancy was plain sailing.

Which is more than can be said for the rest of it. There were all the meetings that I'd been dreading, with social workers, teachers – everyone having their say. I told them I didn't know who the father was, because I didn't want him to get into trouble, and none of them questioned that. Which says a lot about what they really think of me – but they're wrong. I hadn't slept around – just picked the wrong boy to trust, I guess.

We'd been together for a few months, me and Liam. I'd picked up with him when the last foster placement was clearly going wrong. He was kind to me then, and that meant a lot. But it wasn't any great love affair.

"We get on well, you and me," he said, one evening when we'd been having a laugh. "We should stick together."

"What? Be a proper boyfriend and girlfriend?" I asked.

"Well – yeah. We could see how it turns out."

But I knew how it would turn out. We'd stay together for a while and then he wouldn't be able to cope with all the stuff going on in my life – and why would he? I mean, *I* can't cope with it most of the time. So I changed the subject. And pretty soon I could tell he was getting tired of me and my moods, just like I knew he would. Of course, I didn't know about the baby then, but it wouldn't have made any difference.

I don't believe in all that 'being in love' stuff, anyway. You've only got to look around you – Liz is a fantastic person, but she's ended up being a single parent, and look at my Mum. She's never found the love of her life and, let's be honest, she's tried often enough.

I didn't want them to tell my Mum. I didn't want her turning up and making false promises to the baby like all the false promises she's made to me over the last fifteen years. I wasn't going to tell Liam, either. From the start I just wanted it to be me and the baby; he wasn't going to be for sharing. But then Liz talked to me about my Dad.

"You've never seen him," she said. "And if you feel hurt about that, perhaps you should think about how your baby will feel if he never knows his Dad either."

She had a point, but, honestly, I've never met any 18-year-old boy who'd want to be bothered by fatherhood.

But in the end I decided to see Liam. I texted him to meet me at the café where we used to go and I was a bit surprised that he turned up, 'cos it had been ages since we'd seen each other.

When I told him he just kept looking at my bump and saying, "Wow."

"I don't want anything from you," I said. "I just thought you should know."

"Will I be able to see him?" he asked eventually.

I shrugged. "I haven't decided yet. Probably not."

He got a bit angry then. "So why did you tell me, if you don't want me to see him? If you don't want me to be his Dad?" Then he spoke more quietly. "I'd be a good Dad, I really would," he said.

"Yeah, like my Mum was going to be a good mother," I said. "I only told you 'cos Liz said I should. I don't want the baby messed up with people coming in and out of his life like they have with mine. We'll be fine, just the two of us."

And it won't just be us two. There's Liz and Jamie as well. "It's about time there was another male in this house," Jamie said, when the scan had shown it was a boy. The baby will get lots of love and I'm going to make sure I do as good a job with my son as Liz has with hers.

Liz was in care, too, and then brought Jamie up on her own after she split up with his father. It's almost like my life is mirroring hers. She told me all about it one day, when my pregnancy was so far advanced it was making me feel lazy, or lethargic as Liz puts it, and we were curled up indoors together drinking hot chocolate while the rain battered the windows.

"I know it looks like I've found all the answers," she said, "but it's been hard. None of those answers are written down anywhere. The early part, when you're wrapped up in the baby, is almost the easiest, but then it can get lonely. We've been all right, me and Jamie, but I would have liked someone to share it with – the difficult bits and the fun – somebody else to love."

For the first time since I'd been with her she looked really sad. I wanted to ask her why Jamie's dad left, but then the baby started kicking and she put her hand on my bump and we both laughed at the joy of it.

I'm thinking back over those long months as I sit here with the baby. I'm brought back to the present by the door opening. Liz has been quicker than she thought – she probably can't wait to start being a surrogate grandma.

"Time for us to go home," I tell the sleeping baby as I wrap his blanket closer around him.

But when I look up it's Liam's lanky frame filling the doorway.

"What are you doing here?" I ask him. "How did you know?" I hadn't seen him since the day I told him I was pregnant.

"I phoned Liz 'cos I knew the baby was due – I've phoned before, but I asked Liz not to tell you, in case you got upset."

His eyes have been fixed on the baby, but now he looks at me.

"I've got a steady job. To support you both if you'll let me. I've been working really hard. Saved up a bit of money, too. And my parents want to help. Like I do."

I suddenly see it then. Liz was determined that Liam should see the baby, so she's engineered this. I can't believe she's gone behind my back.

"I've got a car outside," Liam says, "I could take you home if you want."

I'm really angry now. This is *my* life, *my* baby – the first time I've had someone to love who is truly mine. Why don't people get that?

"I'm 'phoning Liz," I tell him.

"Can I at least hold the baby, just this once?" Liam

asks.

He's holding out his arms, his eyes pleading with mine. I remember how kind he was when I was so unhappy. He's not a bad bloke. Maybe he's entitled to this at least.

"Only while I make this call," I say, handing the baby over.

I'm keeping an eye on him while I speed dial Liz's number, in case he doesn't hold the baby properly, when I stop dead. Liam's cuddling the baby close and I've never seen such a look of joy and wonderment – and love – on a boy's face before. Maybe my Dad would have looked at me like this.

"You're so beautiful," Liam tells his son. The baby's eyes are open as if he's looking at Liam. As if they are making a connection.

Liam tears his gaze away from the baby and looks at me. The love is still in his eyes. I was wrong, I have seen that look on a boy's face before. I remember it from when we were together. It was me, scared to really trust anyone, who turned away, not him.

My anger fades. Perhaps there's a chance here after all. A chance to be part of a proper family. A first for me and the baby. Wise, wonderful Liz will have seen that all along.

I put my 'phone away.

"All right," I say. "You can take us home. And then we can talk."

His face lights up again. He hands the baby back and pops outside the door. In a moment he's back with a baby carrier.

"I brought it with me, just in case." He grins and I can't help grinning back.

It might not work. We'll both have to try really hard. But perhaps there's room in my life for more than one sort of love. Maybe it's time I started letting it in. And we both should give it our best shot.

For our son.

A Pair of Blue Eyes

The office was buzzing with the news. Vern kept his head down and steadily continued with his paperwork. Around him several voices were raised excitedly.

"What a great idea!"

"I think we can make it work well!"

'Bring your child to work Friday' the email had been headed. It had come from the parent office in America, where such things were an annual event. *'To help everyone to appreciate each other's lives more, and for children to get an understanding of the workplace,'* it had said.

"It'll be such fun!" Tracey, the supervisor from accounts exclaimed.

Fun? Vern thought. The workplace wasn't supposed to be about *fun.* As far as he could see it should be about – well, *work.* It would maybe be helpful for teenagers who were trying to decide their futures, but the company had decreed that all children from the age of three could be included. It wouldn't be so bad if everyone had their own office in which to contain their offspring, but it had also been decided some time ago that open plan offices were the way to go.

He was surprised that some of the men in the company also thought it was a good idea. "It's the school holiday," Neil, who was one of the most successful on the sales team, said. "One less day of childcare to pay for – it'll earn me lots of Brownie points with my wife."

Vern hadn't really thought of what happened to school children in the holidays. He'd assumed, for instance, that Neil's wife was always on hand to look after the children, but now he vaguely recalled Neil saying that she went out to work.

Occasionally babies had appeared in the office, of course. Mothers on maternity leave – and sometimes fathers on paternity leave – proudly brought their new arrival in to show everyone. All the women would cluck around, wanting to give the baby a cuddle and trying to decide if it looked like its parent. From what Vern could tell, all babies looked pretty much the same, and he'd actually feel quite offended if anyone thought a baby's funny, squashed up face and sparse amount of hair resembled him.

He knew people thought his views odd and considered him a loner, so they no longer bothered to invite him to join in such events. But that was fine with him. He had made it clear when he started here that he didn't mix, that he didn't like getting involved in personal stuff. He liked working at his well-ordered desk and gained satisfaction from meeting the deadlines he imposed on himself each day. He didn't feel the need for idle chit-chat.

The talk around the water cooler had evolved into a discussion about turning one of the meeting rooms into a playroom for the special day, with DVDs and puzzles and other games. It began to get on his nerves.

"Lydia," he called over to the young woman who had recently become his assistant, "can you get the latest Morrison figures for me? In case you've forgotten, they're expecting a proposal from us tomorrow."

"Of course – sorry," she said, responding to his curt tone and moving away immediately, which was the catalyst, as he'd hoped, for everyone else to drift back to their desks. Vern chose to ignore the bit of face-pulling aimed in his direction. He didn't really care what anyone else thought of him. He did care about doing a good job.

When the dreaded morning arrived Vern was feeling even more pessimistic about the venture. A recurring dream had woken him in the early hours and further sleep had proved impossible. He had the start of a headache and a pile of work on his desk which had to be completed before the weekend.

It seemed that for everyone else, though, the weekend had already begun. A horde of children of all ages had arrived in the building and there was a general holiday air as parents proudly showed their youngsters where they sat and introduced them to everyone else. Vern was very surprised when Lydia approached his desk with a small girl in her arms.

"This is Grace," she said, "my daughter."

She stood the child on the floor and encouraged her to say "Hallo" to Vern, but the little girl simply viewed him solemnly, her startlingly blue eyes latched uncompromisingly on his face.

"I didn't know," he started to say, his surprise making his voice squeak, so that he began again. "I didn't know that you had a child."

Lydia seemed little more than a child herself, no more than about seventeen or eighteen he'd thought, but she must be a bit older than that to be a mother – mustn't she? He felt confused.

"She's three," Lydia said. "It's made such a difference, not having to rush so much to get her to nursery this morning – and for her not to be waiting for me when I dash back there at the end of the day."

Which explained why Lydia was always so keen to get away promptly at five. Vern had always supposed, that, despite her efficiency, it was a lack of true interest in the job and a desire to be out and about with boyfriends. He'd even been a bit afraid of her ultra-modern clothes and her apparent self-confidence. He hadn't thought of her weighed down with responsibilities.

"Don't you have any family who can help you?" he

asked now, breaking his own rules about personal life intruding into the office.

Lydia shrugged. "My Mum tries to help, but she works full-time too. And Grace's Dad – well, he's not around any more."

"Grace won't be any trouble," Lydia went on, opening the box the little girl was clutching. The box was crammed with Disney figures which Grace proceeded to line up on the floor beside her mother's desk.

Relieved, Vern concentrated on the work in front of him and tried to block out the noise that was increasing all around. The normal buzz of people talking and the ringing of phones was intensified by cries of "No, don't do that!" "Leave that alone!" "Come and see what this is," and even, "Oh dear, we'll have to change your clothes now!"

Grace didn't mix with the other children, however. She stayed close to her mother until the middle of the morning when, looking up, Vern saw her beside his desk. The blue eyes still regarded him unwaveringly, but her little hand was offering him one of the figures.

"Prince Charming," she said gravely.

Lydia looked across and grinned. "You're honoured. Prince Charming is her favourite."

He took it with equal solemnity, said, "Thank you very much," and placed the figure on the corner of his desk. After that from time to time the child returned with various figures and arranged and re-arranged them on the edge of his desk, but Prince Charming remained where he was.

After lunch, things in the office definitely took a turn for the worse. Several of the older children were bored, had no interest in the DVDs on offer, and began to demand more of their parents' attention – whilst their parents began to realise that they hadn't accomplished half the amount of work they should have done, and were now hurrying to complete it. Two of the younger children had tantrums, one began to grizzle through sheer tiredness, and one of the older boys spun round so much on his mother's swivel chair that it fell apart completely and he landed on the floor with a howl.

At this point Vern had had enough. It had been a silly, ill-conceived experiment in his view and it was time for it to stop. He jumped up from his chair with an, "Oh, for goodness' sake! This is a workplace, not a child's activity centre!"

Not used to hearing him speak so loudly or see him move so animatedly, the office came to a standstill.

He swept his arm around. "Look at this place! It's chaotic, and some of us have work to finish by tonight!"

He stepped forward to argue his case more, but at that point heard a crunch underfoot. He looked down. His sweeping arm must have knocked Prince Charming off the desk and now the figure lay crushed under his carefully polished shoes.

Flustered, he bent down to pick it up, while the rest of the office returned to what they were doing as it was clear he was going to say no more.

Prince Charming's left leg was bent and broken and the side of his head was squashed. "I am so sorry," he said, expecting Grace to burst into tears as some of the other children had done. But she just stared at him, with a look of sorrow in her beautiful eyes.

"It's all right," Lydia said quickly, in the cheery voice parents reserve to avert a crisis. "It couldn't be helped. It was an accident – and we know that accidents happen and it's no-one's fault, don't we, Grace?"

Grace nodded and took the damaged figure from Vern's outstretched hand. "It was a little accident," she repeated. "It doesn't matter."

But Vern could see from her face that it did matter. What was worse, he could also see, in a moment of unaccustomed clarity, that here was a child who had already experienced disappointment in her short life.

That evening, in his solitary flat, he couldn't get the child's eyes out of his mind. Eventually he had to acknowledge why. They were the eyes that he saw in his recurring dream. The steady blue eyes of Rachel, whom he'd loved with all his heart. Grace could have been the child there hadn't been time for them to have.

It was dreams of Rachel that broke his sleep on many nights. Sometimes they were dreams that he had let her down; that, if he had done a bit more of he knew not what, she would still be with him. On other nights he would be trying hard to catch up with her, but she would always be a little way ahead of him, tantalisingly just out of reach. She never spoke to him in his dreams, but now he could hear her voice, as steady and warm as her eyes. "Time to let go, love," she was saying. "Time to move on."

Her words seemed so clear he actually looked round to see if, somehow, she was in the sitting room with him. She wasn't, of course, but her words lingered in his head, as loving as they had always been.

On Monday, when Lydia arrived at the office, Vern held out a small box to her.

"It's for Grace," he said.

Inside was a new Prince Charming.

"Please give it to her, with my apologies," Vern said.

Lydia took off the glasses she wore when at her desk. For the first time since she had become his assistant Vern really looked at her. Her eyes were different from her daughter's. They were a deep brown, with little flecks of green, and shadows of something unfathomable. But just as beautiful.

She smiled at him. "That's very kind of you. She loves the way the Prince rescues Cinderella. And I want her to go on believing in fairy stories and happy endings for as long as possible."

Her words sounded wistful and he could sense the vulnerability behind her competent manner. He was surprised at his own sensitivity. Maybe he was beginning to feel again.

Lydia spoke again, her voice diffident this time, "Here's an idea – why don't you come with me this evening to collect Grace from nursery? Then you could give it to her yourself – if you haven't anything else to do, of course."

Rachel's voice was in his head, urging him on, willing him to find a new way without her.

Vern smiled back at Lydia. It felt good. He looked round the office, but no-one was taking any notice of his unprecedented geniality.

"If I do," he answered, "perhaps there would be time for us all to have some tea?"

Lydia looked as solemn as her daughter. "That would be lovely," she said.

The Red Shed

"M rs. Norton!" The warden came bearing down upon Amy like a ship in full sail. "I hope you haven't forgotten the entertainment tonight! Sixty years since VE Day and the war ending – you'll love it, I'm sure! After all, you're one of our oldest residents – it'll bring back so many memories for you."

Amy Norton scowled at the warden. Somehow this woman always brought out the worst in her. "Don't know if I'll be going," she said. "I might have something else on." And before the warden could say anything more, she stomped back into her bedsit.

That was the trouble with living in sheltered accommodation, you were always at the mercy of other people's good intentions. Not that the entertainment tonight wouldn't be good, but there wasn't one of them over fifty – what did any of them know about the war? It would be all *White Cliffs of Dover* with someone dressed as Vera Lynn, and it wasn't really like that.

Amy gazed out of her ground floor window, remembering. Not a bad day, some sunshine. On impulse she put on her coat and hat and found her walking stick. With a bit of luck she'd catch the 11.30 bus.

S he gave a little grunt of satisfaction as the bus turned into the village square and she saw that it was still there. So much was knocked down these days in the dubious name of progress that you couldn't be sure of anything. She leaned heavily on her stick as she moved carefully down the aisle, and smiled benignly to the gentleman who helped her down onto the pavement.

She stood for a moment, looking across the road at the building she'd come to see. No-one else would give it a second glance, of course – there probably weren't many left for whom it would hold such precious memories.

The Red Shed. An uncompromising structure of corrugated iron, painted camouflage green when war broke out, but everyone had carried on calling it 'The Red Shed', and had laughed when the pompous ARP warden insisted on calling it the Village Hall. There was a proper village hall now, standing beside it, a Fifties structure of pebble-dashed concrete and metal windows. But the Red Shed was still there, looking slightly dwarfed by the newer building and possibly a little lop-sided.

She crossed the square and sank down onto a sturdy wooden bench opposite the little building. The spring sun warmed her, and she lifted her face to it, closing her eyes.

She was no longer a very old woman with arthritis and a temperamental digestive system; in her mind's eye she was a young girl again, just turned seventeen, dressed in her best with a shiny new black handbag on her arm, giggling with her friends as she went to her first dance. She'd only been able to persuade her mother to let her go because she would be with Irene from next door, and Irene's older brother Ron would keep an eye on them. She'd been practising her dancing for weeks and was so excited that she'd barely been able to eat her tea.

But after the initial excitement her spirits drooped. Irene, a year older and a regular at such events, seemed to know everyone and was whisked off to dance with first one young man and then another, leaving Amy to sit alone, an increasingly conspicuous wallflower.

Then she saw Arthur across the room, standing near the door, so tall and good-looking that she wondered why every girl in the room wasn't eyeing him in anxious hope. He caught her watching him, so that she'd blushed and half smiled before turning away in confusion. But then he was there in front of her.

"Would you..." His voice sounded at least half an octave too high, and she realised that he was just as shy as she was. He cleared his throat, and tried again, lower this time, "Would you care to dance?"

They'd danced and danced until her feet had ached, so that walking home afterwards with Irene she took her shoes off, and ruined her stockings.

It was all so clear to her. She could see his handsome face now, and her body swayed slightly to the music in her head.

"Are you all right?"

The voice drifted into her thoughts, and as she opened her eyes he was there before her again – her Arthur with his light brown hair that always had a bit of a curl to it, and tender, loving brown eyes. She blinked rapidly and then, as the face came more into focus, realised this was someone she'd never seen before.

"Silly old fool!" she said sternly. "Oh! Not you, lad!" she added quickly as a look of surprise came into the concerned face peering into hers. "It's just that I thought you were someone else."

The lad's face cleared. "I didn't mean to disturb you... I thought perhaps you might be unwell."

"Thank you, but I'm fine. Enjoying the sunshine and reliving a few memories." She bestowed on him the same sweet smile which had captured Arthur's heart so many years ago.

"I usually sit here to eat my sandwiches," he said, indicating the seat. "Will I be disturbing you?"

"Of course not!" Amy replied. "I came to see if the Red Shed was still here – I remember it from over sixty years ago."

He glanced at the old hut she pointed to, and wondered if he should tell her it was green – perhaps she was colour blind. But she'd already turned her attention from him, so he began on his sandwiches.

All through the long hot summer of 1939 they'd danced, or so it seemed to Amy now, and laughed and sung along to *Flat Foot Floogie with a Floy Floy*. Swirling around in Arthur's arms it was even possible to ignore what was happening all about them, but reality struck when Arthur sat her down gently – on a seat very similar to this one – and told her that he'd joined the navy.

His departure was a passionate one, and she hadn't seen him again until a brief spell of leave after Dunkirk. They decided to marry then, and a hurriedly put-together reception was held in the Red Shed.

"Don't worry, I'll be back – turn up like a bad penny," he told her before he returned to his ship. But it was over four years until she saw him again. They wrote to each other frequently, frantically, and after a while she began to send him photographs of his son.

Most of the war years had revolved around the Red Shed. Young Wives' meetings, St. John's Ambulance, dreary 'Make Do and Mend' afternoons when the women sewed and the children played on the floor around them. Taking her mother to Whist Drives, with the Warden fussing about the blackouts in the draughty tin hall. There'd probably be mention of ration books and blackouts at the show tonight, but nothing of the tedium of being a young mother on her own, longing for something more in her life, or the anxiety over whether this would become a permanent state of affairs.

There'd probably be jokes about when the Americans arrived. 'Overpaid, oversexed and over here.' All the films showed them, didn't they – usually called Chuck, tall and handsome with good teeth.

But they weren't all like that. Some of them were slight and shy, with a flop of dark hair and round spectacles. Harry, his name was. Too clumsy and awkward to seek out the girls at the dances at the Red Shed. More comfortable in the company of the young woman who helped with the refreshments. A young woman who would have loved to dance to the foot-tapping music, but was a wife and mother now, so couldn't because tongues would wag and tales would be told when the husband finally came home.

But Harry was glad she didn't dance. He could talk to her of the small mid-West town where he'd grown up, and eventually he told her of his fears when crouched in the rear of the droning bomber in night raid after night raid, that he would never see his town again.

One night, as he helped her stack crates of empty bottles outside the back of the Shed, he told her that he was in love with her, and kissed her, hurriedly, clumsily, and afterwards couldn't stop apologizing for the liberty he'd taken. She was thankful that the dark night hid her blushes, because of how she had so badly wanted to kiss him back.

She didn't see him again.

Then the war was finally over and celebrations overflowed from the Red Shed into the field alongside, with children racing up and down playing games. And Arthur was back! Striding down the path to take her in his arms, with her heart beating so hard she thought it would burst, before lifting up the little boy who peeped shyly out from behind his mother's skirts.

There'd probably be all the songs like *We'll Meet Again* tonight, but nothing about having to learn to love a stranger all over again.

Arthur hadn't wanted to leave the village. "Seen all I want to see of the world," he declared, "and there's nowhere as grand as this!"

So in the village they stayed, watching their son, and later their daughter, grow up. But now it was Scouts and Brownies in the Red Shed, and meetings of the Parish Council on which Arthur proudly sat. Amy would watch him walk down the road towards the Shed, pipe in hand, a slight sailor's roll to his stride, glad that love had indeed come back. And glad that she hadn't told him of the anguish of wondering whether she should have given more to the shy American boy on the night before he died, the boy whose shadow she sometimes saw during the dances at the Shed.

She sighed deeply at so many memories. The young lad beside her looked full of concern again. "It's a bit chilly now – the sun's gone in. Would you like a cup of tea?" He nodded towards a café across the street.

Amy studied him for a moment. "Do you know, I think I would!" She held out her hand. "Amy Norton."

"Danny Archer," he said solemnly, taking her hand and helping her to her feet.

They sat at a window table and Amy told him how much the village square had changed in the years since her husband died.

"You said you remembered the old hut," he asked. "The... er... green one?"

She laughed, a young sound that belied her years. "And you probably wondered what on earth was I talking about when I said it was red!"

She told him, as they drank their tea, some of her reminiscences. She even found herself telling him about Harry. She'd never told anyone before, yet here she was, explaining it to a young lad who reminded her of her husband. Perhaps that was why.

"They still hold dances in the village hall, you know," Danny said, to fill the slightly awkward gap when she'd run out of words. "Sometimes on a Saturday there's a disco and a live band – pretty good those nights are. Not the same as clubbing in town, but it's cheaper. I go most times – with my girlfriend. We like to dance." Suddenly he looked at his watch. "I'm awfully sorry, but I have to go back to work. Will you be all right?"

"Of course," she assured him.

He waved before crossing the square, and she watched until he was out of sight. From the back he reminded her even more strongly of the young Arthur.

How life goes in circles, she mused as the waitress brought her more tea. Danny and his girlfriend, over sixty years on, dancing to all this modern stuff, that probably isn't any sillier than *Flat Foot Floogie with a*

Floy Floy, and making their plans together.

"Mrs. Norton! You've been out so long!" The warden's shelf-like bosom was heaving. "I was starting to worry."

"I told you I had other things on today," Amy replied evasively, closing her door quickly.

If she'd tried to explain, the warden's eyes would have glazed over while she clucked, "Yes, yes, dear," busily, like she always did. She might even look faintly shocked should one of her charges admit to physical pain from old longings that couldn't be assuaged by an aspirin or a visit to the chiropodist.

Amy decided she would go to the entertainment this evening, in memory of Arthur who came home and Harry who didn't. She smiled to herself. Perhaps, when they'd run out of Ivor Novello songs, she might even try to remember the words to *Flat Foot Floogie with a Floy Floy.*

If

*C*rafty little word, isn't it? *If.* So much promise, threat, hurt, love, hope, despair, desire, expectation, wrapped up in that one insignificant syllable.

And all that bargaining power it contains, right from the start.

"If you eat all your dinner, you'll grow into a big strong girl. If you're good we'll go to the park."

"If you do that once more you'll go to bed early."

You get used to hearing it from a very early age. At least, I did. Conditioned by my mother, from as far back as I can remember, to accept conditional love, just as she had. Her face furrowed with fear, her lips cracked and flaky from anxious biting, the list would grow longer as the day wore on.

"If your father sees you doing that when he gets home, he won't be happy. If that mess is still there when he gets in, there'll be a row, you know that. He'll be back soon – if you help me get tea, we'll have a nice evening together."

She didn't realise that, no matter how hard she tried, it wasn't her efforts to placate and appease that influenced my father's behaviour. It was all down to me.

"If I don't tread on the cracks, he'll be in a good mood. If the next car that comes round the corner is red, he won't have gone to the pub on the way home. If I smile

as soon as he comes in the door and sit on his lap the way he likes, he won't notice Mum's nervous tics and get cross... If I stuff my fingers in my ears and sing in my head I won't hear the fighting when I'm in bed. If I breathe really slowly and pretend to be asleep when I hear him on the stairs then perhaps he'll leave me alone tonight. If I promise to keep our secret, like he says, he'll look after me."

If I think about it now, I can see how unfair and untrue the word was all through my youth. All through the months and years when I struggled to break free of the shame that imprisoned us all. That's when the word held so much promise.

"If you work hard and do your best, you'll pass your exams and the world will be yours" – Yeah, right. All very well for teachers to say, locked into their regulated lives, where to expect homework delivered pristine and on time isn't unrealistic. No mention of how difficult it can be to do your best perched at the end of the table littered with the remains of the evening meal, with the television blaring and no-one prepared to make any concession for what you are trying to achieve. Until you get to the point where you are just too exhausted from making all that effort to no avail.

Yet I yearned so much for the promises to come true.

"Come on, babe, if you really love me, then show me. You know how much I care about you. If you want to be my girlfriend, you'll do it – everyone else is."

The old, old *if,* that one, isn't it? I wonder how many other girls over the years, starved of real love and affection, have fallen for it, and then fallen in other ways.

Then there's all that Kipling Boy Scout stuff. Such a lie. All those 'ifs' might work to make you a man one day, but what if you're a woman and you're tired of 'holding on'?

I could have held on through all the *if only's* – the uncertainties, disappointments and apparent bad luck – if those loving, imploring, pale blue eyes hadn't changed to ice chips, impervious to reason, as soon as lust was replaced with familiarity.

"If you didn't nag me all the time, I wouldn't lose my temper. If you didn't spend all the housekeeping so quickly I wouldn't be so stressed! If you kept the kids quiet of a night, I wouldn't lash out, would I?"

And afterwards, all passions spent, when a tiny piece of remorse would filter like daybreak over the wreckage of our marriage... *"If you give me another chance, it won't happen again... promise."*

If I'd been stronger on the first occasion, if my craving for the love of another human being hadn't blinded me, if I hadn't taken the easy route of false hope every time, if I hadn't accepted that the fault was always mine, I might still have all my teeth.

Our meagre bags are packed. We're ready. If I can keep my nerve and we leave now, then maybe he won't find us. The children deserve more than this – no, what did my mentor tell me? *I* deserve more than this. If I can keep her calm, caring voice in my mind, I might keep my resolve.

The taxi's here. A necessary extravagance, because someone might see us get the bus and report back. There's that old lady across the road, always watching from her window. Not that she'd have anyone to tell, I don't think. But there are others, eager to share a snippet of information from the same lips that remained firmly sealed, along with eyes that refused to see when a little compassion, a little help was needed.

The driver kindly carries our few belongings down the path, his cheerful chatter needing little response, which is just as well as I am speechless with anxiety. I wait nervously as he folds the buggy into the boot, irrationally expecting to see a figure come hurtling down the road towards us, shouting and swearing, even though I've timed it all so carefully. If the man will just hurry up we'll be gone in good time.

I slam the front door shut, with no looking back. If this works I can close the door on my past as well and really start afresh.

Kayleigh's little hand trustingly, unquestioningly, placed in mine gives me strength. I hold the baby tightly in my arms as we set off. If I can give them both a better life than they've had so far, then hopefully their short past will be blotted out too, and this terrifying step into the unknown will have been worth it.

Huddled in the back of the taxi, the baby still in my arms and Kayleigh snuggled in close, I give the address when the driver turns in his seat to ask where we want to go. If this refuge is a rescue for the soul as well as the body, I can be a whole person again and provide for these two small beings who asked for none of this.

The driver, the same sort of age as the father I haven't seen for years, looks at me thoughtfully for a moment, nods once and gives a little smile before turning back. I may be wrong, but in that smile was a wealth of understanding. He's seen it all before, and his complicit smile tells me that I'm doing the right thing, the only thing. He doesn't say anything but leans forward and switches his meter off. For a moment, within my thudding heart, there is a brief surge of joy that this act of goodness, of rare kindness, is a sign. A sign that, in time, our lives will be good.

If there is a God, I hope he's with us now.

Hay Fever

$\mathcal{M}$r. Gotley? Hallo, I'm Sheila Frazer. Do come in. Thank you for coming out to see me. Won't you have a drink?

"I'll come straight to the point. As you may know, we bought this house through Manning and Gotley – let me see, it must be all of twenty-six years ago, when your father was in charge of the business of course, so it seemed only right that we – I – should use you now it's time to sell it.

"'Mmm – it is a beautiful property. It's very dear to me... so much has happened here over the years. But times change, Mr. Gotley. As I said to you over the 'phone, I'm on my own now – it's alright, I don't need condolences, it's not a bereavement. I'll be frank with you. My husband has found... has decided... no, no, I'm not upset, just the eyes watering a little – hay fever, you know. As I was saying, my husband has left me – there, I've said it now – and he's – we've – decided that it would be best to sell the house and go our separate ways.

"Thank you Mr. Gotley, you've been so understanding. I'll leave it all in your capable hands."

$\mathcal{M}$r. and Mrs. Fowler? Hallo, I'm Sheila, do come in and I'll show you round. No, no you're not late, the estate agent said three o'clock. Now, shall we start with the lounge?

"Yes, it is quite spacious – plenty of room when our three children were growing up. And then we had the conservatory added through here – somewhere for my husband and me to have a bit of peace when they were teenagers! The place was always full of their friends. Home from home, they used to say.

"My husband? Oh... he's... er... he's... working away at present – up north – yes, we'll probably move up there when the house is sold. Here's the dining room... and through here is the kitchen. Have you used an Aga before? You soon get used to it, and it does seem to make the kitchen the heart of the house. We... I... spend most of my time in here. No, we've not had any firm offers yet – the house only went on the market last week. It will be a pity to leave it after so long, but there we are... I'm sorry... I must just find a handkerchief... would you like to look round upstairs on your own?

"Thank you, I'm fine now, just a touch of hay fever I think. Did you see everything you wanted to upstairs? Good. Well, if you want to come back at any time, just let the agent know."

Katie? Ah, found you in at last! I've phoned a couple of times during the last few days. Didn't you get my messages? Yes, I know I could have sent a text, but you know I don't like them. How are you, darling? Oh, I'm fine... managing quite well, really I am. How is the studying going, darling? I do hope this dreadful business won't affect your exams.

"Of course I don't mind you seeing your father – he is still your father, whatever has happened. Well, I'm sorry if he doesn't seem very happy, but it really was his choice, you know, I didn't make him leave. No, of course you haven't upset me, darling. It's just that having turned us all completely upside down, I don't want to hear that your father still isn't happy – he seemed quite delirious when he left. Anyway, don't let me drone on about my problems. How are things with you...?"

*M*r. and Mrs. Burroughs? Hallo, I'm Sheila. Do come in and I'll show you round. I'm glad you found the house all right. The lane is so leafy at this time of year it hides the house numbers. Now, where would you like to start? The garden? Yes, of course. I always think it looks its best in June.

"Thank you! The roses are my favourite too, especially the climbing ones over the pergola. My husband usually – I mean used to – buy me a new bush every wedding anniversary... I shall miss them.

"No, no, don't worry, you haven't upset me, really! Hay fever playing up! The truth is, we're separated... getting divorced actually, so I need somewhere smaller, especially with going back to work again. This is your second marriage? Oh well, you know how complicated it all gets. But I'm sure I'll manage – and you both look happy enough, I must say! Shall I show you inside now?"

*S*tanton 6329... Liz! How good of you to call. It's all right, I know you're busy – thought the Stanton grapevine would soon fill you in with what's been happening, though.

"I think I'm over the worst, now. Seem to be 'getting my act together', as they say. Of course it was a shock, but I should have known. She's been working in his office for months, and looking back there had certainly been a chasm growing between us. I think we had stopped really talking to each other. And, as seems to happen, the wife was the last to know.

"Everyone has been very kind. Claire keeps popping round to cheer me up – she's very into this counselling business at the moment, isn't she? She brought me a book about the male menopause yesterday. She's quite convinced that that is Bill's problem – I didn't like to say that I thought his problem was small and blonde and definitely not menopausal!

"Oh, yes, I'm hanging on to my sense of humour. And you're right, I have to be more assertive. I've made a start – at least now I look people in the eye and tell them that I'm getting divorced. I'm almost beginning to believe it myself!

"No, truly, it doesn't upset me to talk about it any more. It's just the wretched pollen count – sets my hay fever off. Thanks for phoning, Liz."

*M*r. and Mrs. Smith? Hallo, I'm Sheila. Do come in and I'll show you round. And who's this young man? William! What a lovely boy! That's all right, do let him run about. It's good to hear a child's voice again. This house was made for children, he won't come to any harm.

"We had three ourselves. All left the nest, now, of course, but they still come home when they can. Our youngest was born in this bedroom – I'd got fed up of hospitals by then. He was a summer baby – I used to sit down there on the swing chair on the patio – you can see it from the window here – and feed him while the other two ran around. That rhododendron bush over there was their den – they'd spend hours playing inside it. Yes, it is a home full of memories...happy ones... but listen to me going on! Let me show you round the rest of the bedrooms.

"When is your next baby due? October! Oh well, you'll be wanting to move in good time for then. No, there's no chain involved here. I can move out at very short notice. I've found a little flat on the other side of town, and it's already empty. Doesn't have a garden, of course, but there is a balcony. It's amazing what you can grow in pots and tubs these days. I might even manage some miniature roses..."

*M*anning and Gotley? Hallo, this is Sheila Frazer here, could I speak to Mr. Gotley please? Well could you ask him to call me back, please, when his meeting has finished? It's been a few weeks since anyone has been to look at the house."

*H*allo Mr. Gotley. Thank you for returning my call. No, you haven't caught me at a bad time – just this wretched hay fever. No, I haven't been taking any medication – this is the first time I've suffered from it. About the house – do you think we should lower the price? I've just come back from a visit to my solicitor, and he seems to think the quicker we get things sorted out the better.

"'Mmm – I think a five thousand drop is perfectly reasonable, but I'll have to consult Bill first. I'm afraid I'm not sure of his address at present – I'll ask my solicitor to contact his solicitor. Thank you Mr. Gotley."

*M*r. Wilson? Hallo, I'm Sheila. Do come in and I'll show you round. Has Mr. Gotley told you that the price has been reduced? Oh, there's nothing wrong with the property I can assure you; I – we – just want a quick sale, that's all. Well, if you're in the building trade, Mr. Wilson, you'll be able to see for yourself that the house is in good condition.

"I suppose the fourth bedroom is a bit small, but it has a lovely view of the garden. Does your wife enjoy gardening?

"The loft? Yes, of course. If you'd like to pull on that hook there, the ladder will come down. That's it! No, I shan't be re-decorating before I go. That would be up to you, of course – nobody ever shares the same taste, do they? But we rather liked these light colours.

"The whole house has definitely been re-wired – it was a few years ago – I've got the guarantee somewhere.

"The plumbing has never been a problem, Mr. Wilson. I'm sure the pipework is standard. My husband has always seen to that sort of thing. He's not around for you to call back later, I'm afraid, he's left m– the area!

"I think if you want to know all these details you would need to have a survey done. No, nobody has ever told me that the bricks need re-pointing – and they've not said anything about the window frames rotting or the drains blocking up!

"I'm not becoming hysterical, but I'm sorry, if you want to see any more you'll have to call back again – my hay fever, you see, affecting me dreadfully at the moment! Well, for your information, Mr. Wilson, it can still play up when it's pouring with rain!"

Stanton 6329. Oh, Bill! It's you! Of course it's me! I probably sound a bit muffled – I've got hay fever... I know I've never had it before, but there's a first time for everything.

"I wasn't being churlish contacting you through your solicitor. I only had your office number, and I wasn't going to phone you there.

"Yes, I'm fine, apart from this wretched hay fever. Are you alright?... Good...

"Was there something in particular you wanted, Bill, only I have to go out in a minute. I've an interview for a job. You said I ought to get out and about more. Nothing very exciting, unfortunately. Filing and clerical work – it seems my secretarial skills have become a bit rusty over the years.

"Well, the offer's only just below what we were asking. I suppose we have managed to sell it rather quickly, after all. Pleasant young couple called Smith. They said they can just afford it now we've dropped the price. They think the house has a nice family feel. They've got a lovely little boy called William and another one on the way. I'm glad they are going to have it. It will be rather like when we moved in, won't it? ... They remind me of us all those years ago... they seem very close... oh damn! Here I go again! I just can't seem to stop my eyes streaming. Sorry, Bill, I'll have to go! I'll be late for my appointment."

Katie? Won't keep you long, darling! Just wanted to share my good news with you – no, it's nothing to do with your father. Even more amazing – I've got a job. And it's better than I thought. It's at 'Faraway Places', the travel agents. Of course it's all computers now, but that's not a problem – they're going to give me three weeks intensive training to get used to their systems – and I thought it was simply going to be a bit of clerical work. They liked my manner apparently – said I was a 'people person'. Fancy!

"Thank you, darling, I knew you'd be pleased for me."

*H*allo again, Mr. and Mrs. Smith – or can I call you Anne and David? Come along in, I've just made some tea. Now you have a look at whatever you want. After all, it will be your home as soon as we've exchanged contracts. Why don't you come with me, William, while Mummy and Daddy are busy doing all their measuring up. I've been fetching boxes down from the loft, and I've found all sorts of toys – all the things my children used to play with – I'd forgotten there was so much up there... I don't know what I'm going to do with them when I leave here"

*H*allo Mr. Gotley, sorry to bother you. It's just that the contracts seem to be taking rather a long time to be exchanged. I wondered if there was some sort of problem that you might be aware of – all that my solicitor seems able to find out is that the contracts have been sent to all the parties. Yes, I gather that my husband has yet to sign – but he hasn't been in touch with you about any delay? It's strange, apparently he doesn't seem to have been in touch with his solicitor very much either, lately. Oh well, I'll be glad of a bit longer in the house. What with working and trying to keep up with the garden, I haven't got round to doing much about packing."

*L*iz? It's Sheila. Just wanted to let you now how assertive I'm being! The children keep visiting me as if I'm some sort of invalid, and then can't believe how well I'm doing!

"And the job is fascinating! I wish I'd done it years ago. You should see me in my business suit!

"I'm even thinking of arranging a nice little holiday for myself once this ghastly business is over.

"A lot of this is down to your good advice, you know. Thanks Liz."

Oh, Bill! It's you! Yes, yes, I suppose you can come in. I'm sorry the place isn't very tidy – the children each came over yesterday and were sorting out their bits and pieces, and I've been out all day to-day. Didn't I tell you that I got the job? Oh yes, it's wonderful. I'm meeting so many new people. Hence the new hairstyle. It's so much easier to manage like this when I'm dashing out in the mornings. And of course I had to buy all sorts of new clothes.

"I'm sorry, I didn't realise I was 'gabbling'. What do you mean you don't want the house sale to go ahead? It's all arranged – at least it will be when you sign the contract. It was your idea, after all – you said I'd never be able to manage here by myself.

"You seem upset, Bill. Sit down and I'll make some coffee. I really don't think we ought to argue about this. We've managed to stay completely civilised so far.

"What did you say? Oh, now look what I've done! Coffee everywhere – no, leave it, I'll clear it up later. Did I hear you correctly? You want to come back? But I thought you were setting up home with Melissa? Well, I know I've always thought she was an empty-headed little thing, but you said you were in love with her.

"Oh, no, you're not an old man – although I think I'll have to agree about the foolish bit.

"I don't know, Bill. You've put me through so much. I can't just go back to how it was and pretend nothing's happened.

"Oh, darling, don't get upset. I can see that it wasn't easy for you to come round and talk to me like this – you've always been such a proud man. But I have my pride, too.

"Of course our marriage meant a lot to me, but I can't simply about-turn every time you fancy a change, you know.

"I'm not being flippant, but when you left here you said it was because you'd changed – 'moved on' I think was the term you used. Well, I've moved on as well, now, Bill. I've moved on, moved into the world again, I'm even facing up to moving out of this house, which I never thought I would be able to do, and I must say I rather like the person I've become. And I don't think I want to go back to being the person I was!

"No, I'm not getting upset. This rotten hay fever just flares up at the most inconvenient times. Yes, I will give it some thought, Bill, but I really think you'll have to go now."

*L*iz? It's Sheila. Sorry to bother you, but I'm feeling in a bit of a mess. No, it's not the divorce. Well, it is and it isn't – Bill wants to come back, and I think I could do with a bit more of your assertiveness therapy.

"You're right, I know, I should stick to my guns and lead my own life now, but honestly, he looked dreadful. I don't think his shirt had seen an iron.

"Yes, I know some men will twist things round to get their own way, but I never thought Bill was like that.

"Could you come round, do you think? Thanks, Liz, you're a gem."

*H*allo Bill. Come in. Thanks for answering my message – messaging's a godsend when you haven't got a secretary, isn't it?

"I wanted to tell you that I've been thinking a lot – about what you said the last time you were here. And I think that if we give it another try – no, no, wait! I only said 'if' and I haven't finished yet. You might not like it when you hear the rest! If you come back, I – well, I've got a list here:

"I'm not going to give up my job.

"And I would want us to go out more – have more interests together. This travel agency where I work has really opened my eyes. I've come across some wonderful bargain breaks I fancy – a week-end in Paris or Amsterdam sounds nice... Oh, dear, where was I? Oh yes:

"And you try never to go into the office on Saturdays. And we stay in this house, which I know is too big for us and we rattle around in it a bit like peas in a drum, but after all it is our home, and all those roses in the garden will remind us of what we've meant to each other, and one day there will be grandchildren, and after all with two of us working we could afford some help and...

"No, it isn't hay fever this time. I'm crying because... Oh dear! This isn't how it was supposed to go at all! Liz will be furious with me! I 'm supposed to be telling you that I want more respect for the new woman I've become, but nothing is sounding how I meant it to... and what I really want to say is that I've never stopped loving you!

"I'm scared, though. I 'm sure you mean it when you say you'll make it all up to me but...

"Thank you, I would like a handkerchief. Then we can talk about this very carefully. No, I don't think you ought to put your arms around me...

"Oh, Bill!"

Hallo, Mr. Gotley? Sheila Frazer here. I'm sorry, but we're not going through with the house sale after all. Bill... my husband... you see, he's back... we're going to stay together and try again. I'm sorry to disappoint the Smiths, but they are young, there'll be another house for them.

"No, I don't think we want to make a fresh start somewhere else. Everything we want is here, and this house – well, it holds all our history, with far more good times than bad. We couldn't take that with us. All the reminders of what we've shared together over the years will help to hold us together if things get a bit difficult at times.

"Thank you, I thought you would understand.

"My hay fever? Do you know, now you mention it, it's completely better!"

The Sandwich Filler

*H*ave you noticed how every time you go anywhere, people are obsessed about what job you have? As soon as you're introduced, they're asking, "And what do you *do?*" That's why I was dreading the reunion. Not old school friends this time, brought together by yet another foray into *Friends Reunited.* This one was a nursing reunion – one which we'd all pledged to attend in the heady aftermath of passing our finals twenty years ago. And there are some people who never give up on this sort of thing aren't there? Theresa Phillips-that-was, she was the one in our group who sent an annual newsletter round and tracked down old members even when they'd fled as far afield as Australia.

Anyway, I'd promised my friend Paula, the only nursing friend I still kept in touch with, that I'd go with her to this reunion, but I knew what it would be like. As soon as people recognised you and had finished sizing you up to see if you'd put on more weight or got more crows' feet than they had, they'd ask the dreaded question, "And what are you doing now?" And I knew, from those newsletters, they'd all be high-flyers. The London hospital where we trained back then had been a bit like an upmarket girls' boarding school where the headmistress expected her 'gels' to get on in life.

I thought about telling them that I'm a sandwich filler,

which is what I tell those market research people who stop you in the street. Not your usual sort of sandwich, though. I'm the filling slapped between two truculent adolescents and an elderly mother, who between them keep this single Mum firmly fixed at home, battling to keep both sides of the sandwich apart.

The children tease me that I'm a worse telly addict than their generation because the TV's always on when they come in from school. But it's for Mother, really. She's an ex-librarian who loves all those afternoon quiz shows and it's good for her to keep her brain active, especially as her arthritis keeps her body pretty inactive. I keep her company through reruns of *Millionaire* in the evenings when the kids are doing homework or seeing their friends. But during the day I'm sort of aware of all these programmes as I go about my chores, although it's the adverts that stick in my mind more than the answers to the quiz questions. Shame the afternoon ads seem to be predominantly about getting rid of ear wax, or coping with faulty dentures or constipation – have they ever thought those last two could be linked? That's the sort of thing I think about when I'm ironing and imagine that I could write a nursing paper on the subject.

Anyway, I made a big effort for this reunion, because I'd already decided that it would be the only one I would ever go to. I'd managed to lose some weight and grabbed a very slimming outfit in the sales, with a cute pair of high heels. The children had agreed to look after Grandma without squabbling with her or each other, and I'd arranged to meet Paula at London Bridge, so we could go to the hospitality suite of our old hospital together.

The shoes were my downfall, though. Literally. There isn't much need for high heels when you're at home most of the day, so I was out of the habit of tottering along in them. And out of the habit of remembering that they could get caught in pavement grids. The heel of my left shoe snapped right off as I neared the station and I went lurching across the pavement. Luckily only my ego was bruised, but the shoe was ruined.

Then I remembered that ad – you know the one – where the same thing happens to a bride and a page boy turns up with some superglue. Of course, there was no page boy for me, but further down the road I could see a hardware shop and it looked as if it might still be open. I checked my watch – nearly six o' clock – took off my other shoe and galloped down the road.

"Please don't close yet," I gasped to the man who was clearing the items displayed on the pavement, "I need some superglue." Although from the way I was huffing and puffing I sounded more in need of oxygen.

But Bob – he was the actual owner of 'Bob's Hardware Store' – was kindness itself. He sat me on a chair in the shop and listened to my tale of woe. "You'll have to wait a few minutes, for it to harden," he told me, holding the heel with its layer of glue firmly onto the shoe, "but it should do the trick and you'll still have time for your train."

While I was waiting I found myself telling him all sorts of other things – I think I was still heady from my unaccustomed sprinting – until he said, "I think this is ready now."

Then he fetched me a glass of water while I tried the shoe out for sturdiness. I couldn't thank him enough and set off for the station as sedately as possible.

By the time I met Paula I was calm and in control again. "I nearly didn't make it," I began to tell her, keen to share my little anecdote as it was the most exciting thing that had happened to me in ages.

But she wasn't really listening. As we left the station she grabbed my arm. "I've been thinking about this place such a lot since this reunion was planned," she said, "and guess what? I've signed up for a return-to-nursing course – right here, back in our old hospital!"

We joined the other 'old girls' for a whistle-stop tour of some of the wards and departments, exclaiming at the changes since our day, in between eyeing each other up to see who'd changed the most. As we walked round I felt a pang of envy over Paula's plans as waves of nostalgia swept over me for our heady, ambitious, younger selves and the satisfaction that nursing had given me.

It was later, half-way through the finger buffet, when I remembered. Trudie Jennings-that-was had been telling me about her exciting life married to a prostate surgeon. I couldn't contribute much to the conversation, not having a husband or a prostate, so my mind wandered a bit. I was surreptitiously moving my left foot back and forth to see if the heel was still firmly fixed when it came to me in a flash – I hadn't paid for the glue! All that kindness and I'd simply waltzed off with just a "thank you very much".

I flushed when I realised, so much that Trudie obviously thought I was going through an early menopause because she quickly passed me on to Lorraine Barker-that-was who is now a sister on a gynae ward.

I went back to the shop the next afternoon, leaving Mum grappling to find nine letter words on *Countdown*. I'd carefully rehearsed my apology, so I was quite disappointed to see just a young girl behind the counter.

"Sorry," she said when I asked for Bob, "but he's gone over to the other side."

Used to my mother's speech being peppered with euphemisms, for one dreadful moment I thought she meant that he'd died. She must have noticed my blank look because she quickly said, "It's our second shop – on the other side of town." My disappointment that he wasn't there was even more acute than my relief that he was still in the land of the living. I explained to the girl about the glue and gave her my money.

I had my head down when I left the shop, wondering how I could spin out the time until Mum had watched *Pointless* as well, when there was a voice behind me. "Hallo, how did last night go?"

Now I can't remember the last time I propositioned a man – divorce and being a sandwich filler doesn't leave you with that much confidence or give you much opportunity. But one of those coffee ads was in my head, where the couple are in that 'will they, won't they' situation, so before I realised it I was saying, "Have you got time for a coffee and I can tell you all about it?"

"Lots of the girls I trained with are still in the profession and doing really well, and here's me doing nothing very much at all. So I came home feeling quite disgruntled that I'm not doing something more worthwhile with my life," I told him over cappuccinos at a nearby café.

He was really understanding, because it turned out he's a bit of a sandwich filler too. Wedged between his daughter – the girl in the shop – and an elderly father, Old Bob. We spent quite a lot of time comparing notes over a second coffee and he didn't try to tell me that I should be trying to find fulfilment in my life as it is.

A few days later Bob brought Old Bob round to challenge my mother to a game of Scrabble. In a weird role-reversal we hovered in the background like two parents who've arranged a play-date for their offspring. Luckily they hit it off really well, even though my mother wouldn't allow him to put in swearwords and he questioned some of the obscure words she put down to get rid of her awkward letters. They play Scrabble a couple of times a week now, and Old Bob has also persuaded Mum to accompany him to a day centre on Tuesdays and Thursdays.

And what do I do now that I've got some free time? If this was really like the adverts on the telly, there ought to be one of those happy endings where Bob and I got on so well that this was the start of a lovely romance. But Bob is happily married to Annie, who shares the care of Old Bob. They both encouraged me to get back into the work place. Paula's back-to-nursing course was still out of the question, time-wise, but I've managed to get a part-time job at our local cottage hospital, assisting the dietician. There's a lot of contact with the patients, which I love, and I've had to hone up about different aspects of nutrition. Which is enough of a happy ending for me at the moment while I've still got two lively teenagers and an elderly mother to think about.

And sometimes, when the ladies in the hospital kitchen are really busy, I put the fillings in the sand-wiches!

Red Shoes

I t was the shoes Vince noticed first. The tip-tapping across the laminate floor of the reading room was brisk enough to make him look around from his game of chess. The sound was being made by a smart pair of red high-heels. Moving his glance upwards, he saw that the wearer of the shoes was a slender woman with curly hair pulled into some sort of topknot from which a few tendrils had escaped. A gash of red lipstick to match her footwear added to the brightness of her face.

She was being ushered into the room by Mrs. Blake, who never wore high-heeled shoes and was a sturdier shape altogether. A comfortable, reliable woman – just the right type, Vince always thought, to be the warden of a retirement complex. But she now had retirement plans of her own, which involved moving to the Lake District to be nearer to her daughter.

"Ah! I thought I'd find you two in here," Mrs. Blake said, as they approached the table where Vince and Phil always sat. "This is Mrs. Harvey, who is taking over from me. But perhaps you would both like to join the rest of us in the main room, so that I can make the formal introductions?"

The woman probably wasn't so many years younger than Mrs. Blake, but she seemed to be of a different generation. She smiled at them. "It's Rachel. And please, don't stop your game on my account. I hope to be meeting everyone personally over the next couple of days."

Phil smiled back at her. "It's no problem," he said, deftly moving a chess piece, "because it's my move – and I think you'll find that's checkmate!"

Vince looked down at the board suspiciously. He hadn't seen that coming before he turned away, but this was no time to challenge Phil's triumph. There was nothing for it but to concede defeat, in every way, and to follow the two ladies into the large sitting room.

It was already crowded with what seemed to be nearly all the residents. Tea and coffee were being dispensed, cups and spoons clattering amongst the buzz of chatter. It was the sort of gathering Vince really disliked and he silently cursed himself for forgetting that this was the morning they had all been summoned to meet Mrs. Blake's replacement. If he had remembered, he would have foregone his regular chess game with Phil and stayed in his airy flat.

The chess games were the only forays he made into the community building. The rest of the time he was content with his own company, reading, or simply watching the ever-changing river which he could see from his window. That way he could cling onto his independence and convince himself that he didn't need the support that the retirement complex offered.

Now, he accepted a cup of coffee from one of the ladies, whose names he never remembered, and decided he would stay just long enough to be polite. As long as his way of life stayed the same he really didn't care too much who was in charge and this new woman, in her clickety-clackety red shoes, seemed pleasant enough.

But things didn't stay the same. Mrs. Blake had kept everything on an even keel, called everyone 'dear', and made sure people like the chiropodist made regular visits to the complex.

But Mrs. Harvey – Rachel – had other ideas. Within weeks she had organised make-up and fashion events for the ladies – "you don't have to wear elasticated trousers once you turn 60", she'd announced – and even Vince couldn't help but notice that soon several of the ladies had new, more youthful hairstyles and manicured nails painted in strong colours.

Then she turned her attention to activities. "This large room is so under-used," she said, "especially in the afternoons." Before long there was something going on every day.

At least, to Vince's relief, she left the reading room alone, so his games of chess with Phil continued as before. But sometimes she would pop in to ask them if everything was all right.

She didn't always wear clickety-clackety shoes when she was working. Often she was in soft shoes so it would be a few minutes before Vince realised she was there, watching the game intently and waiting for a pause in their concentration before speaking.

"I notice that you don't seem interested in any of the other activities here, Mr. Kennedy," she said to Vince once day. "I thought you might have come along to the short mat bowls afternoons – they're proving very popular. I've even managed to persuade Mr. Lawson here to join." She indicated Phil, who smiled back at her.

"I've tried to persuade him, but he's too stuck in his ways," Phil said.

Vince liked the way she called him 'Mister' – that didn't happen very often these days – so he tried not to sound too gruff. "I'm not one for joining in things – I'm quite happy with my own company."

"I can appreciate that," she said, "but there was something that I'd hoped you would help me with. I want to start up a book club and reading group, and I've been told you are probably the best-read person here, so I wondered if you would come along and choose the first book for everyone to read?"

"Sorry," he said, "but I'd prefer not to."

He turned back to the chess game, moving a piece

with great deliberation so that he didn't see her wait for a moment before leaving the room.

"Your turn," he said to Phil. But Phil sat back in his chair with an exasperated sigh.

"You miserable beggar!" he said to Vince. "Can't you see the effort that she's making to stop us all from just stagnating? Haven't you noticed the change in the place – it's come alive in the last couple of months, and it's all down to her. And it can't be easy for her when she has to deal with miserable old goats like you."

"I can't help it if I like being by myself," Vince said.

"Well carry on, then," said Phil, laying down his king to concede the game, "because I'm off to the meeting about the stately home trip next week."

Vince sat for some minutes before heaving himself out of his chair with a sigh and making his way to the little office where Mrs. Harvey – Rachel – was sitting, frowning over some papers. Her frown was quickly replaced by her wide smile when she saw him in the doorway.

He cleared his throat. "About the book group – I've had a think. I'll give it a go. I'm sorry, you know, about just now... I find it hard since..."

As his voice tailed away he saw her glance at a photo above her desk of a handsome man.

"Don't worry – I know it's difficult, isn't it, when you're suddenly on your own..." Her smile had taken on a certain wistfulness. "But – I'm so pleased that you've changed your mind. Thank you."

They talked for a few more minutes about when the group should meet and about choosing a suitable first book that would be both stimulating and engaging. Walking back to his flat, Vince realised that it was the longest conversation he'd had with a woman for the best part of five years.

He was surprised at the success of the first meeting. People whom he'd barely bothered to say 'Hello' to turned out to have all sorts of interesting points of view, and he found himself enthusiastically joining in the discussion.

"I enjoyed that more than I ever thought I would," he said to Rachel afterwards as they tidied the room. "Thank you for encouraging me to do it."

She nodded. "My pleasure – and now there's something else you can do in return. I'm starting an afternoon tea dance next week, you may have seen the notices about it. Oh don't look like that until you know more about it," she said as she saw his face fall. "It's just that I need all the men to turn up and give it a go, so that the ladies won't end up dancing with each other the whole time."

The wide smile was there again. "Go on – give it a try, just for me. You never know, you might enjoy it as much as the book club!"

"I'm sorry, but I don't dance –"

"That doesn't matter, you can just be there to make up the numbers of men. Then, if you want to, you can always learn. Please? Just for one time?"

Somehow he found himself agreeing, but as the week wore on he felt a sense of dread every time he thought about it. On the afternoon itself he might have chickened out completely had Phil not knocked on his door to see if he was ready.

The large room was beautifully done out with pretty tablecloths and delicate china transforming the rather functional tables. Rachel was in the midst of things as usual, wearing the red shoes that he remembered from her introductory visit. Vi and Frank, who told everyone they were just good friends but were clearly becoming an item, had joined in immediately and were urging others to have a go.

Vince sat uncomfortably at a small table with Phil, making sure he was eating a cake or drinking some tea every time he thought a lady was looking meaningfully in his direction. Phil, though, succumbed in the end, whisked away by a lady who patiently took him through the steps of a slow waltz. Vince wished he could go back to his peaceful apartment and sat looking at the floor, planning his escape, when he saw the red shoes in front of him.

"I know you said you don't dance, but I've danced with every other gentleman in the room, so I've decided we must have one go at it before you run off!"

He looked up into her teasing eyes. How had she known what he was thinking?

"Come on," she said, holding out her hand. "My shoes have been ruined with so many toes treading on them, but this is a foxtrot – it's not too hard, I'll show you."

He closed his eyes for a moment. It had been over five years. He took a deep breath, opened his eyes, stood up and took Rachel in his arms. If he hadn't been feeling so emotional he would have laughed at the surprised look on her face as he whisked her expertly around the room.

"I thought you said you couldn't dance!" she spluttered when the music ended.

"No – you interrupted me," Vince said, "when I'd been going to say that I don't dance since my wife died – we used to go every week, but it wouldn't have been the same after she'd gone."

He couldn't bear the stricken look on Rachel's face, so before she could say anything he went on, "But now you've got me on my feet – how are you at the quick-step?"

She smiled, "You lead, I'll follow."

She danced well and for a few minutes it was like he had his Gwen in his arms again – a bittersweet memory, but not as painful as he'd imagined it would be.

"Thank you," he said, when the dance finished. "I enjoyed that."

"So maybe you'll come again next month?" she asked.

"Maybe I will," he said, but this time his habitual gruff tone was softened.

He thought a lot about dancing with Rachel over the next few days. The memory of her steps matching his and the feel of her hand on his shoulder kept intruding when he was trying to read his book, and the fragrance of her came, unbidden, into his head when he was trying to enjoy his view of the river. He told himself he was being a silly old fool. He would go to the next dance just to be polite, that was all.

But just before the next tea dance could take place there was suddenly no more Rachel. Mrs. Blake reappeared, "to fill in, until Rachel is back on her feet."

The official line was simply that Rachel was on sick leave and would be returning as soon as possible, but rumours abounded: *she'd had major surgery; she'd had a breakdown; she was having chemotherapy; she would be back soon; she was never coming back.*

Flowers and cards were sent by concerned residents but they were told that she didn't want any visitors.

All Vince knew was that the place wasn't the same any more. He'd been spending more time in the community centre lately, sometimes over a coffee with someone from the book group, and he'd even let Phil persuade him to try short mat bowls, which proved to be much harder than it looked. What he hadn't realised was how aware he'd been of Rachel flitting about the place, her energy and cheerfulness combining to create a sense of wellbeing without ever becoming overpowering. He missed the way that, if she was in the same room, he would be aware of her presence, even when she was talking to someone else. And he realised, now, that he had formed a habit of waiting to catch her eye so that she would bestow her smile on him. He also realised that he didn't want to be called 'dear' for the rest of his life.

Eventually they were told that Rachel was back in her warden's flat, but that she still wouldn't be returning to work for a while so Mrs. Blake would be staying in the visitor's suite and running the place for a bit longer.

Fed up with the fresh round of speculation this news sparked, Vince cornered Mrs. Blake in the little office.

"I won't go gossiping, " he told her, "but I want to know how Rachel is, and whether or not she's coming back, because if she isn't there are things around here that need sorting out."

Mrs. Blake seemed to understand that here was a resident who wasn't going to accept platitudes. She put down her pen with a sigh.

"The thing is, dear," she said, "she's been given the all-clear, and could really be back here – and goodness knows that would help me because I've got a grandchild on the way – but it's more to do with her confidence. It's as if she hasn't got the will to face everyone again."

"Then we'd better do something about it," said Vince.

The warden's flat was down its own little corridor, so it was easy to make sure that no-one noticed him as he approached Rachel's door. She gave a surprised 'Oh!' when she answered his knock.

"I know this might seem like an imposition, but that's what you did to me when you first came here – imposed yourself when my life was quite orderly as it was," he said, in rather a rush so that she wouldn't close the door again, "so you can't complain if I'm doing the same to you."

There was the ghost of a smile in a face that was paler and slightly sharper-featured than before, with new faint lines around the eyes that spoke of pain. Without a word she led the way into her little sitting room.

"We need you back," he said. "Apparently you're well enough."

He waited while she struggled to find the words.

"I – I... it's just..." She raised her eyes to his and he saw that the pain wasn't physical any longer. "I've had a breast removed," she said. "I'm not the same person – I don't feel the same, I don't look the same."

"It happened to my Gwen, too," he told her, "only she was never lucky enough to be given an all-clear. She felt devastated at first, said it made her less of a woman."

He leaned forward, "But she never stopped being beautiful. Or funny. Or kind. Or feminine. It never changed the woman she was inside – all the things that made her loveable, and you are all those things too. They are what people see."

"How can you say that?" she whispered, "You hardly know me."

"But I know how everyone has missed you, and how you brightened up all our lives, and how we all want to see you again. For us you'll be the same Rachel with the curly hair and the wonderful smile and the personality that cheers us all up."

"Including you?" she asked.

He nodded solemnly. "Including me."

"And I also know what a good dancer you are," he went on. "Gwen and I started dancing after she had her operation – she said it made her feel like a young girl again. She said it was better than any therapy."

He opened the carrier bag he'd brought with him and pulled out a box.

"So this is for you," he said, "Not a 'get well soon' present, but a 'come back to us' present."

She opened the box. Inside was a pair of red, strappy shoes.

"You said your others were ruined from everyone treading on your toes," Vince said, "so Mrs. Blake told me your shoe size and I bought these to ask you to come to the next tea dance."

Rachel took out one of the shoes and stroked the soft leather.

"They're lovely," she said. She looked back at him, her smile a little more certain this time, and a ray of hope in her eyes.

"Will you be there to dance with me?" she asked.

Vince felt his heart begin to swell with love for the first time in five years.

"Every step," he said.

Today's The Day

Today is the day you're going to leave me. I can sense it. If I'm honest I've been aware that this day has been coming for weeks. Something about your manner, your lack of interest in anything I say to you, your reluctance to join in with the things the rest of us are getting up to.

And sometimes I've caught you with that far-away look in your eye as if you're thinking about where you're going, who you'll be meeting and what you'll be doing. Of course, as soon as you've become aware of me watching you your expression has changed. You've tried to hide it. You've forced a smile and an artificial brightness and begun some sort of trivial conversation. But it hasn't fooled me. Not one little bit.

A couple of weeks ago I caught you scribbling furtively in a notebook, which I've not seen since. Your financial arrangements, perhaps? I've wondered if I should snoop around a little, discover your intentions. But then I might find out more than I want to. And I'll find out soon enough after you've gone. I know, whatever happens, that you wouldn't leave us with nothing.

Not that I haven't probed a bit, though. But you're not easily caught out. And every time I ask if there's anything bothering you, you give me that reassuring smile and, "No, of course there isn't. Nothing at all. I'm fine." But beyond the smile there's a determined set to your face that stops me pressing you more. Somehow it's not as easy to talk these days.

It hasn't always been like this. Do you remember when Daniel was born? The excitement, the joy? How you went round knocking on all the neighbours' doors, telling them, "It's a boy! It's a boy!"

We had so little money then and I was desperately worried about how we'd cope. But you never stopped being positive. "We'll manage, together," you said, and there was so much love in your eyes for the two of us, that you gave me the confidence to believe you.

We worked hard, though, didn't we? What a team! You'd get in at the end of a long day in the office and I'd go off to my night shift at the hospital. You never minded looking after Daniel – changing him, feeding him, playing with him. There was that long, hot summer when he was small and I'd switched to day shifts at the weekend. I'd come home to find you both in the garden, playing tennis. Daniel with a racket that was almost as big as him, insisting that he was Bjorn Borg and you were McEnroe. You were almost as excited about telling me of your day together as he was.

You rescued him from my natural inclination to be an over-protective mother. I can see you now, after you took the stabilisers off his bike, running alongside him up and down the pavement, your hand resting lightly on the saddle, as you urged him on. "That's it! Good boy! You can do it." It took some time, but eventually he was cycling on his own without even realising it. You staggered back into the house afterwards, your face aglow with satisfaction, but holding your sides as you caught your breath. "Ooh," you groaned, "I'm going to have to get fitter than this. He'll be wanting football coaching next."

You started on a healthy eating kick after that, but I'd often come into the kitchen and find you sneaking an extra piece of your favourite cheese out of the fridge and you'd make me laugh with your outrageous excuses. There was so much laughter in those days, despite all the struggles.

It's funny, looking back, how those little, imperceptible changes crept in over the years, for both of us. Somehow, as Daniel grew up, we grew a bit more apart. Each of us becoming more wrapped up in our own affairs, our own jobs and interests. Sometimes we would bicker over Daniel, especially during the difficult teenage years.

"You let him get away with murder," I'd tell you, while you would grumble: "You're too hard on him. You should let him have a bit more freedom." And yet we managed to rub along together, didn't we?

There were times, however, when I would catch you daydreaming and the guilt would send prickles down my spine. I'd always known you had plans and dreams that were never realised because you'd stuck to your principles when we found out I was pregnant.

"We'll cope with this," you told me. "It may not be what either of us had thought was going to happen in our lives just now, but we'll be fine. You'll see."

I've never loved you more than I did then. The dreams were resolutely packed away and barely mentioned afterwards.

Sometimes, though, as the years went by, I wondered if this was what you really wanted. Or if Daniel and I should move out, to let you live the life I felt deep down you were pining for. But then you'd come up with some plan for a holiday that we could just about afford if we were really careful and your eyes would sparkle with all the old mischief. We'd sit on some sunny beach, or walk for hours along twisting lanes and you'd suddenly stop in the middle of a conversation, suck the fresh air into your lungs and drink in the beauty of the surroundings and say, "Look at this! Isn't it wonderful! Life can't get any better than now, this moment, here." So I would convince myself once again that you were happy with this choice, this life.

It wasn't that amicable all the time, of course. We had some fights along the way, as well. Once was on that holiday in Italy when you and Daniel had gone for a swim in the sea while I ordered lunch at the little beach-side café. Do you remember? I'd dropped all my change in the sand and a man, tanned and romantic-novel handsome, already sitting at the bar helped me to pick it all up and then bought me a drink. When you came back with Daniel you took an instant dislike to his smooth Latin ways, your hostility making sure he didn't hang around long. After he'd gone I accused you of being rude, while you accused me of flirting.

"Lucky I came back when I did, he was obviously trying to pick you up!" you'd said.

"No he wasn't, he was just being kind!" I retorted. "And anyway, even if he was trying it on, I'm quite capable of looking after myself!" Your raised eyebrow of disbelief had infuriated me even more, and we didn't speak for the rest of the day. Dinner that evening in the restaurant when Daniel was in bed was a stilted affair with me smiling winningly at all the waiters, just to infuriate you. Looking back I can see that at that time you were as unsure about me as I was about you. There have been other times during recent years when I've thought this day had arrived. But I fought for you each time, determined that you weren't going to leave me, that I could make you stay. And you did, even if our relationship shifted a bit.

It's not the same today. There is a different look about you and you're further away from me than you've ever been. Deep down I know that whatever fight I put up isn't going to change anything. And maybe it wouldn't be fair anyway. Maybe now is the time to let you go. To move on without me.

But nothing will stop me loving you, you know. Part of you will always be with me in some way – how can it be any other after all these years? And then there's Daniel. He has such a look of you and so many of your mannerisms: a constant reminder of how things once were. I'll keep reminding him, too, of the good times, so that he'll think of you in the best way. No recriminations, no 'what ifs' or 'if onlys'. That wouldn't be fair.

You're facing away from the door as I come into the room. Everything is very still and quiet but you don't turn at the sound of my footsteps. I'm not going to falter at this lack of reaction, though. If today is the day, if this is the moment when my life is going to be turned upside down, then there are some things that have to be done properly.

I take hold of your hand. Despite my good intentions I can't help myself saying, "Don't go. Please stay," but I say it so quietly, barely a breath, that perhaps you don't hear.

I wasn't going to cry, either. I was going to maintain a dignified control, but suddenly there are tears streaming down my face. Part of me wants to lose it altogether, to let out the anger that you are deserting me. I want to scream and shout at the unfairness of it all to unseen deities, "I don't want it to be like this! I want to turn the time back, have things like they used to be, when we were all happy together!" Before there was this gnawing anxiety inside me that I was going to be left alone.

I bite hard on my lip until the flow of tears is stemmed. Then, in a louder voice, so that you can hear me no matter what, I say, "I love you so much."

But it's almost too late. Your hand has gone limp in mine.

Good-bye Mum. Rest in peace.

About the Author

*J*ulie has been a successful short story writer for magazines and competitions for two decades, in between writing four novels, pantomime scripts, songs and scripts for adult and children's drama productions, and features for national and regional newspapers and magazines.

Her working life began as a nurse and health visitor, and she undertook a range of occupations whilst bringing up her four children, from being matron at schools where her husband was headmaster, to being Town Clerk in her home town of Usk in South Wales, teaching piano, and running a successful drama company with her daughter, which she continues to do.

Julie's first novel, *The Mountains Between,* is set in her beloved Monmouthshire, telling the story of two very different families living each side of the Blorenge mountain during the difficult years between 1929 and 1949. It has been a regional bestseller.

Her second novel, *Just One More Summer,* is a modern story set in Cornwall and London, and, as well as being popular in this country, is now being published for the German market by a Random House imprint.

Julie returned to wartime South Wales with her third novel, *Don't Pass Me By,* which tells the heartrending story of a group of evacuees sent to a remote Welsh village.

In recent years Julie has become something of a

campaigner, successfully heading a protest group to save the local library, and organising a 100,000-strong petition for better cancer treatment in Wales. Her passion for people informs her fiction writing, and her interest in health and social issues triggers much of her non-fiction writing.

In her spare time, as well as reading and gardening, Julie loves spending time with her family and her ever-growing band of grandchildren, and playing tennis.

She also enjoys giving talks about her books and writing to a diverse range of organisations and running writing or drama workshops at festivals.

If you would like to know more about her writing, or to invite her to speak at a gathering, take a look at her website: www.juliemcgowan.com, or email Julie on juliemcgowanusk@live.co.uk – she would love to hear from you!

The following are sample chapters from
Julie's first three books:

The Mountains Between
Don't Pass Me By
Just One More Summer

THE MOUNTAINS
BETWEEN

A searing and powerful novel from
one of Wales' best-loved authors

Julie McGowan

The Mountains Between: Sample First Chapter

Part One

1929 ~

Jennie

Jennie heard Tom's voice calling her, but she ignored him and scrambled over the gate into the ten-acre field. She ran head down, forcing her legs to go faster and faster, her breath coming in great racking sobs, until she reached the corner of the field where the land sloped down towards the railway line, and she would be hidden from the house. As she flung herself face down onto the grass and the sobs became bitter, painful tears, Mother's words echoed in her head, refusing to be quelled.

You were never wanted! You were a mistake!... A mistake... a mistake!... Never wanted...!

The day had started so well. The Girls were coming home and Jennie had been helping Mother in the house – as she always did, but more willingly this time, excitement tightening her chest because her sisters would soon be here and the summer holidays would then have begun in earnest. Mother, too, seemed happy; less forbidding, and the crease between her brows that gave her such a disapproving air had been less pronounced.

Never wanted!... A mistake... Your Father's doing!

Eventually there were no more tears left to cry, but the sobs remained; long drawn out arpeggios every time she inhaled. And the more she tried to stop them the more it felt as if they were taking over her body.

She sat up and wrapped her arms around her knees in an effort to steady herself. A small girl dressed in a starched white pinafore over a blue print summer frock, with two mud-brown plaits framing a face whose eyes looked too large for it. She stared at the mountains – her mountains, her friends, keepers of her secrets. But today she wasn't seeing them, could draw no comfort from the gentle slopes of the Sugar Loaf which stretched out like arms to encompass the valley. Today the mountains were majestic and aloof, wanting no share of her misery. In her head the scene in Mother's bedroom replayed itself endlessly before her.

She'd been returning a reel of thread to Mother's workbox – a sturdy wooden casket kept in a corner of the bedroom. Inside were neat trays containing all Mother's sewing things, and one tray full of embroidery silks, the colours rich and flamboyant as they nestled together. Jennie had lifted the silks up and let them run through her fingers, enjoying their smooth feel and the rainbows they made.

Then, for the first time, she'd noticed that what she thought was the bottom of the workbox was, in fact, too high up.

She lifted the rest of the trays out and pulled at the wooden base, which moved easily to reveal another section underneath. There was only one item in it; a rectangular tin box with a hinged lid on which was a slightly raised embossed pattern in shiny red and gold. She traced the pattern with her fingers. It was an intriguing box. A box that begged to be opened.

Jennie had lifted the tin clear of the workbox when suddenly Mother appeared in the doorway, her face bulging with anger.

"What do you think you're doing? Put that down at once!"

Taken unawares by her mother's arrival and the harshness of her tone – excessive even for her – Jennie turned suddenly and the box had fallen out of her hands, the hinged lid flying open and the contents scattering over the floor. Had she not been so frightened by Mother's anger, Jennie would have registered disappointment, for the box, after all, held only a few old papers.

To Mother, though, they seemed as valuable as the Crown Jewels. With an anguished cry she'd pushed Jennie aside and scrabbled on the floor to retrieve the documents.

"I'm s-s-sorry," Jennie stammered, "I didn't mean ..."

But Mother wasn't listening. She was too busy shouting.

"Why don't you ever leave things alone? This is mine! You had no business! You're always where you're not meant to be – always causing me more work! Either under my feet or doing something you shouldn't!"

Her voice had grown more shrill as she spoke, with a dangerous quiver in it, so that Jennie didn't dare offer to help – or to point out that the things her mother was accusing her of were grossly unfair. She'd given up doing that a long time ago. "... It's not right – I didn't want... Three babies were enough!"

Mother had been looking down, thrusting the papers back in the box, continuing to exclaim about the unfairness of her lot as she did so, almost as if she were no longer addressing Jennie. But then she'd snapped the box shut and swung round to face her daughter.

"You were never wanted, you know! It was all a mistake! All your Father's doing!" She turned back to the workbox, her shoulders heaving with emotion.

There was a moment's silence.

"What did Father do?" a crushed Jennie had whispered.

Mother's hand had swung round and slapped Jennie across the ankles. "Don't be so disgusting!" she'd hissed. "Get out of here!"

Jennie knew, as she sat on the grass, that Mother had meant it. She was used to her mother's tempers, her insistence that the house, the family, and at times the farm, were run exactly as she wished, but this was different. The expression on her face as she'd spoken the dreadful words was one that Jennie had never seen before. It had been full of a strange passion – and something else which Jennie, with her limited experience, couldn't identify. But it had frightened her.

Never wanted! A mistake!

It changed everything. Nothing in her world would ever be the same again. Her eight years thus far had been secure ones; lonely at times, being the youngest by so many years, and hard when Mother's standards were so exacting. But happy, too. Happy in the knowledge that she was well-fed, clothed and housed; well-cared for (didn't that mean loved and wanted? It appeared not). Happy on the farm, surrounded by her mountains, and in the company of her beloved father.

Father! Jennie's heart beat faster in alarm. Did this mean that he didn't want her either? That he too saw her as some sort of mistake? Her relationship with her mother always held uncertainty, but Father's affection never seemed to waver.

A kaleidoscope of images of herself with her father rushed through her mind. Making her a wheelbarrow all of her own, so that she could 'help' him on the farm, when she was only four. Holding her in his arms when she cried because a fox had got in and wreaked havoc in the hen-house; comforting her because she'd been the one to discover the terrible decapitated remains. Letting her help to make new chicken sheds, safely off the ground – not minding when she'd splashed creosote on the grass. Urging the cows to milking, his voice kind and gentle, calling each cow by name and helping her to do the same until she could recognise each one.

Surely he loved her! He had to love her!

Panic was rising inside her and she wanted to run to her father and beg him to tell her that it wasn't true; that she wasn't simply a mistake. But fear stayed her. There was the awful possibility that he might tell her even more dreadful things that she didn't want to hear. It would be the same if she asked The Girls, and as for Tom, well! – he had never disguised the fact that a sister six years younger than himself was fit only for endless teasing.

The words were still playing in her head when suddenly the panic eased. What else had Mother said? ... *All your Father's doing!* She didn't know what her father had done, but surely if he'd done it then he must have wanted her?

She lay back on the grass and closed her eyes. Perhaps if she went to sleep she would wake up and everything would be just as it was. She could go back to the house and carry on as usual and the lead weight in her chest that was making breathing so difficult would be gone.

The hot July sun soothed her. Mother would be cross if her skin burned, but Mother being cross about such a thing didn't seem quite so important at the moment. Convincing herself that her Father loved her and wanted her was, she instinctively knew, the only thing that would help her to push her mother's awful words to the back of her mind.

Katharine Davies sat on the edge of her bed, her shoulders sagging uncharacteristically, her breathing rapid and shallow. The papers were safely stowed away again but the episode had unnerved her too much for her to return downstairs just yet. Jennie was too young to have understood the implications of what the papers contained, but what if she told the older children of their whereabouts? A hot flush spread over her anew as she considered what they would think of her. She tried hopelessly to calm herself, but memories of nearly seventeen years ago refused to go away.

"Edward! Oh Edward!"

The voice was her own, urgent, pleading as his hands caressed her, explored her; and she wasn't urging him to stop. Oh no! To her everlasting shame she wanted him to go on, to satisfy the craving that had taken over her whole body. And he had: gone on and on until she felt she was drowning; until she had screamed her ecstasy.

I love you Katie. I'll always love you! Edward had held her afterwards, murmuring into her hair, promising to take care of her. And he had. But it hadn't been enough.

The memories sent prickles of shame up her spine until her neck was on fire. Yet, unbidden, the feeling was there again; that same burning physical wanting that had gnawed away at her in those early years, trapping her with its demands, its insatiability.

She stood up abruptly, angry that her body should be betraying her after all these years when she'd thought she had it firmly under control. She clenched her hands tightly in front of her. She must, she would, maintain that control.

She forced herself to think of what must still be done, which chores in the dairy or in the garden would best exercise her treacherously unreliable body.

She thought fleetingly of Jennie as she moved swiftly out of the bedroom. She shouldn't have spoken to her as she did, but doubtless the child would get over it – would probably look at her with those sheep's eyes for a day or two and then it would pass.

But you meant it, nagged the mean voice of Conscience.

She clutched the crucifix hanging round her neck, as if gathering strength to push the voice away. *I'll pray about it tonight,* she vowed, making for the stairs.

"Bessie! You'd better see about scalding the milk or it will turn in this heat! Then come and help me clean the dairy."

The girl, plump and homely, turned from the large stone sink where she was peeling potatoes, ready to make a cheery remark until she saw the expression on her employer's face. Best not look in the churn, madam, she thought, or the milk will turn never mind the heat.

Jennie saw her mother in the dairy as she entered the back of the house and tiptoed up the back stairs. She didn't want Mother to see the grass stains on her apron.

She'd thought long and hard once she'd finally stopped crying, and had decided that if she tried, really tried, not to let Mother see her doing anything wrong, and not to argue with her ever again, then perhaps Mother would forget that she was 'a mistake' and decide that she was the best-loved and most wanted of all her children.

She sighed as she reached her room. It would be hard work. There seemed to be so many things that Mother had definite and immovable views on. Take her apron, for example. Aprons weren't meant to get dirty. Mother's aprons always stayed spotless – except for the apron she wore over her apron to do 'the rough'.

Not that Mother ever did the really dirty jobs. They were done by Bessie, the latest in a long line of girls who stayed until they could take Mother's demands for perfection and her sharp tongue no longer.

She put on a clean apron and went to the recently-installed bathroom to wash her hands and face, careful to wipe the basin clean afterwards and replace the towel just so. The bathroom was a sufficiently new addition to be treated with exceptional respect. Then she returned to the kitchen by the front stairs so that Mother would think she had been in the house all along.

"May I go now, please – to meet The Girls?"

Jennie didn't want to look Mother in the face; instead she fastened her gaze on the shiny gold crucifix.

The crease between Mother's brows deepened as she surveyed her daughter. She opened her mouth as if to speak, but closed it again. Then her shoulders dropped a little as she appeared to relent from whatever it was she had been going to say.

"Very well. But wear your sunbonnet – and keep your apron clean!"

Jennie went meekly to the little room behind the kitchen and fetched her sun hat before letting herself out through the back door, forcing herself to walk sedately in case Mother was watching her as she crossed the farmyard – immaculate as ever because the cows weren't allowed to cross it lest they make it dirty.

Once round the corner of the barn she ran again to the gate of the ten-acre field. But she didn't climb over it this time. Instead she divested herself of her apron and sunhat and hung them on the gatepost before turning to a smaller, iron gate which led to the lane running parallel to the field.

She began to skip along the lane, sending up little clouds of dust as she went. It was impossible, somehow, to walk once you were out-of-doors and alone, even when you were feeling pretty miserable. Had she been feeling happier she would have tucked her skirts up into the legs of her knickers and tried a few cartwheels. But as she thought this, the awful words bounced up at her in time to her skipping... *Not wan-ted... not wan-ted... not wan-ted...*

The engine hooted as it pulled out of Nantyderry Halt, diverting Jennie. No need to think about anything else now The Girls were home! She broke into a run as they appeared at the end of the lane. They were each wearing their school uniform and carrying a small case; Tom would take the van down later for their trunks. Their uniforms bore the badge of the convent school at Monmouth, which they attended not because they were Catholic but because it was the best school in the area, and they boarded, not because it was far away but because that was what the best families did.

Jennie threw herself into the arms of her eldest sister, sure of a rapturous response.

"Steady on!" laughed Emily, swinging her round. "You nearly knocked me over! Let me look at you! You've grown again while we've been away! Laura! Don't you think she's grown?"

Laura, a year younger than sixteen-year-old Emily, but inches shorter and already more buxom, hugged Jennie more steadily.

"At least an inch taller," she agreed.

"Does that mean I can use your tennis racket this summer?" Jennie asked excitedly, turning back to Emily. "I've been practising like mad against the barn wall with the old one, and you promised me yours when I was big enough."

"We'll see," came the reply. "You'll have to show me how good you are."

But Emily's eyes held a merry promise and suddenly she caught hold of Jennie and danced round with her again.

"Isn't it wonderful? I've finished school for good! My very last day! I can hardly believe it!"

"It won't be so wonderful if we're late for dinner," Laura reminded her, picking up her bag and beginning to walk up the lane. "Jennie, your dress is terribly dusty – Mother will have a fit!"

"It's alright," said Jennie, "I can cover it up with my apron – I've left it on the gate."

But as they reached the gate, there was Tom, Jennie's sunhat perched ridiculously on his head, and the apron held aloft.

"Give it back, I mustn't get it dirty!" Jennie cried, hers arms flailing wildly as Tom held her easily at bay with one gangly arm.

"Please, Tom!" Laura sounded as urgent as Jennie, as the gong for lunch sounded from the house. "You know she'll get into trouble."

Emily sauntered through the gate behind her sisters. "Give her the apron and the hat, Tom, and carry these bags in for us." Her voice sounded almost lazy, but Tom was aware of the authority behind it. He was taller than both his sisters, but Emily always managed to make him feel small.

He relinquished the garments to a relieved Jennie, tweaked each of the long brown plaits hanging over her shoulders, and then grinned. "Better not spoil the homecoming, I suppose."

But he didn't move to embrace his sisters. Instead they all hurried in for dinner.

Come along! Come along!" said Mother as Father stopped to kiss and hug his two elder children. "This dinner will be getting cold."

Jennie contrived to sit between Father and Emily and at once felt happier, although tears threatened again when Father asked her in his gentle voice what she'd been doing all morning. Fortunately Mother began speaking to Emily, and as it was unwise to talk at the same time as Mother she didn't have to answer.

Edward Davies surveyed his family with a degree of pride as they sat round the large, scrubbed kitchen table. All four children well-grown and healthy – no mean achievement when you compared them to the malnourished rickety children over in the valleys, many of whom would be lucky to survive infancy. He would have liked another boy, for the farm, but he loved his daughters nevertheless.

Not that Katharine would have been happy with another boy – there'd been enough fuss as it was when Jennie came along, so he'd thanked God that He had seen fit to bless them with another girl. For some reason Katharine saw girls as a blessing and boys as a kind of blight. *Poor thing,* she would say whenever she heard of a mother being delivered of a son, no matter how longed-for. She treated Tom well enough for all that, Edward allowed, although he never saw the look of pride in her eyes that he had seen other mothers bestowing on their sons. But then, he reflected, Katharine was not like other mothers in a good many ways.

He watched her now, talking to Emily. She was still a

handsome woman, despite her nearly forty years, with no hint of grey in the coils of rich brown hair which she wore piled high like Queen Mary. She'd kept her figure too, which was petite, with delicate wrists and ankles, but her body had always curved in and out in the right places.

Beautiful she'd been, when he first met her; beautiful with no idea of her beauty, which was what he'd found so appealing. Large grey-green eyes, more green when stirred to anger or passion, had beguiled him, and a relentless determination to set the world to rights according to her own view of things had been particularly attractive in one who looked as if she should languish and be pampered all day.

They first met when she was only eighteen, and had returned home from being a children's nanny to care for her younger brothers and sisters following the death of both their parents – her father having discreetly drunk himself to death after losing his wife from septicaemia.

Edward had watched her over the next few years as she struggled valiantly to prepare her siblings for adult life, while he himself was struggling to make a go of his first smallholding. But it had been some time before he'd plucked up courage to court her formally; there had always been an elusive quality about her that held him back, whilst at the same time tantalising him. She was twenty-three before the demands of her family had ceased and she had begun to take Edward seriously and allow him any degree of familiarity – and then, to his joy, what sensuality had been unleashed! And he had loved her! Oh, how he had loved her!

And I still love her now, he mused sadly. But it had been many years since the passion which had simultaneously driven and mortified her had been given rein. The determination which had enabled her to take over successfully from her parents had been channelled into 'getting on' in the world – or at least in the important bits of the society in which they moved, while the passion had been supplanted by a strange mixture of worldliness and godliness.

And, he thought with a sigh, *if cleanliness really is next to godliness, then she'll have a special place reserved for her when she gets to the other side.*

 END OF SAMPLE CHAPTER
*"The Mountains Between" by Julie McGowan
can be purchased from all good online stores,
or better still, ask for it from your local independent
or chain book store.*

About

THE MOUNTAINS BETWEEN

Despite its physical comforts, Jennie's life under the critical eye of her tyrannical mother is hard, and she grows up desperate for a love she has been denied. As she blossoms into a young woman World War II breaks out. Life is turned upside down by the vagaries of war, and the charming, urbane Charles comes into her life – and he loves her ... doesn't he? ...

On the other side of the scarred mountain, in the wake of a disaster that tears through his family and their tight-knit mining community, Harry finds the burden of manhood abruptly thrust upon his young shoulders. He bears it through the turmoil of the Depression years, sustained only by his love for Megan. But his life too takes many unexpected turns, and the onset of war brings unimaginable changes. ... Nothing is as it was, or as it seems ...

Blaenavon and Abergavenny surge to life in this vibrant, haunting, joyful masterpiece – a celebration of the Welsh people from the 1920s to the 1940s. It's the saga of two families and their communities, and the story of two young people who should have found each other much sooner. It's the story of the people of the mountains and the valleys who formed the beating heart of Wales.

*The Mountains Between became a regional best-seller almost immediately. Now in its 3rd edition, it was author Julie McGowan's first book, and is based in her much-loved homeland of Wales. Her second book, **Just One More Summer,** is a wonderfully intricate read based in Cornwall, while her newly-released third book, **Don't Pass Me By,** is also a Welsh spectacular.*

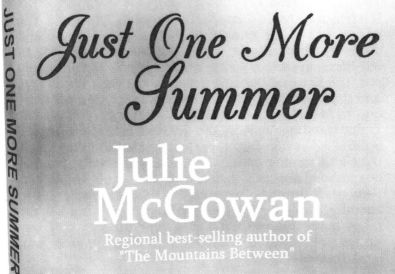

Just One More Summer

Julie McGowan

Regional best-selling author of
"The Mountains Between"

Just One More Summer:
Sample Chapters

Chapter One

Okay ... Let's get this straight right from the start. First, this is not yet another story about a nearly thirty-something who is looking for the right man to whisk her down the aisle and spends every working minute agonising over how she'll meet him, or crying because she thinks she's already found and lost him. And spends every non-working hour trowelling on the make-up and propping up a bar in the hope that tonight will be the night, and if it isn't she may as well take the best on offer anyway ... I mean, is this *really* what women have been fighting for, for the last three decades or more?

Second, there won't be any talk of designer labels – except by my mother, perhaps, although she's more into Mondi and Jaeger than Gucci and Chloe. It's all very well if you've got a nifty little job in advertising or the media – which you've somehow obtained by default and miraculously managed to keep, even though you can't use the computer properly and you spend an inordinate amount of time in the ladies' loo. But it's entirely different if you're secretary to a solicitor and the new kitchen units still have to be paid for. The nearest I've ever got to designer clothes is a pashmina of doubtful origin and a pair of Nike trainers in the sales – although at least my underwear's H&M rather than M&S. Even I draw the line somewhere. Third, I haven't got a tumbling mass of red-gold curls which become engagingly unmanageable at a hint of rain; green eyes, skin that has to be shielded from the sun, or a honed and toned body. Think smallish, darkish, straight hair, trim enough body because I walk a lot, and a complexion that turns dirty brown in the heat. An appearance which my mother, had she been born fifty or more years earlier, would have called 'common', but which she now concedes grudgingly at least allows me to get a tan without staying in the sun long enough to get wrinkles.

Oh yes, and I haven't got the statutory stunningly handsome but gay best friend with whom I can indulge in a bit of mutual shoulder-crying when our respective boyfriends let us down. I'm sure it's all to do with the solicitor's office being on the wrong side of the river – Purley, or at least my bit of it, just doesn't seem to abound with men who have 'come out'.

And while I think of it, there won't be lots of F-words scattered about either, to inject a bit of realism. Yes, I know it's supposed to be everyone's favourite expletive these days, but quite honestly it hasn't infiltrated my part of sedate suburbia to that extent yet. True, Will used it a few times when we were having a mega-row, but that really was in extremis – and I did have one good friend who had a fondness for the word, but I hardly see her these days. Will didn't really like her, you see, so our friendship sort of petered out. And why didn't he approve of her? Because of her foul mouth apparently, which he didn't like in women ... which more or less proves my point, I think. Or else it's the dreary world of solicitors' offices to blame again – I don't mix with people who dare to be so bold.

I haven't even got a handsome but scary boss whose taciturn manner disguises the fact that he is rapidly falling for the darkish looks, straight hair, etc etc, along with my endearing stupidity. Mine is portly and avuncular and breathes heavily from defective sinuses, not passion. Or at least he did up until yesterday, when he ceased to be my boss.

Because as from yesterday I am no longer a solicitor's secretary, just as I am no longer a wife. Now I am an ex-secretary and an ex-wife, soon to be divorced, sitting on the floor of what will soon be my ex-flat, wishing my mother hadn't shown up just at this precise moment.

At this point in my life I really could have done with a mother who wasn't quite so composed, so smart, so *sophisticated,* as mine. Come to think of it, there were lots of times in my life when I would have preferred my mother to be one of those homely bodies who gave out lots of good advice without sounding too much like Claire Rayner and was always there with a comforting bosom to cry on. This was simply another of those times.

She was standing, small – that's the only similarity between us – and elegant in crisp cream linen, with a look of distaste on her face as I crammed a few more T-shirts into my already overstuffed bag.

"But *Cornwall!*" she kept repeating, as horrified as if I had said I was off to war-torn Baghdad. "Why *Cornwall?*"

"Because I've had enough of London and I need a break – which is exactly what you told me I needed several weeks ago."

"For the *whole* summer? Allie, darling, what on earth will you *do* there?"

I pulled a strap tight on my suitcase and turned back to her. "Very little I hope. At first, anyway. If I do get bored or short of money, I'm sure I can get a job in a pub or something just for the season – or I might decide to stay there forever; I don't know."

"But why not something more exotic? Crete, or somewhere – lots of sun and plenty going on?"

"And plenty of men ready for a short summer fling which will help make me feel wanted again?"

My mother ignored the sarcastic tone in my voice. "Well, it wouldn't be such a bad thing, would it?"

"Yes it would. I've told you, I don't want to meet anyone else – and definitely not some holiday Romeo whose brain is in his trousers and is only interested in a quick wham-bam-thank-you-ma'am."

Juliet (she'd insisted that I call her by her Christian name after she finally divorced my father when I was twelve and was hoping to find a younger man – even going so far as to knock a couple of years off my age as well as hers when necessary) had stayed in a villa in Lindos during her first honeymoon in 1970, high above the little town's only burgeoning disco. So she refused to believe that any of the Greek islands would have changed since then, and winced at my choice of phrase.

"But *Cornwall*," she persisted as I continued to arrange luggage all around her. "It will be full of families and will probably rain for most of the time."

I sighed and stopped what I was doing so that I could face her squarely. She clearly hadn't remembered, and I wasn't going to remind her and get into a conversation which would begin: *Ah, yes, your father ...* and then be full of barbed comments which I didn't want to hear again.

"But it will be *normal*," I said instead. "I don't want a fairy-tale existence for a few months in an artificial setting surrounded by artificial people, because I'd still have to face reality afterwards. And jetting off abroad is no fun on your own, and even if I had someone to go with – which I haven't – I would be lousy company and just spoil their holiday as well. *You* told me I should have a break," I went on quickly before Juliet could say, *but I'll come with you darling if you're going to be lonely,* "and that I should get away from it all, so I'm doing exactly as I'm told." I forced a bright smile. "So you ought to be very pleased that your advice is being taken. Leave me to get on with it, and go back to your Floral Society and all those men who want to make an honest woman of you at the Conservative Club."

It was Juliet's turn to sigh. "Well, if you're sure ..." she began doubtfully.

"Of course I'm sure," I said, more positively than I actually felt because I didn't want Juliet to say *but Cornwall!* again. "And if you really want to help you can keep an eye on this place for me while Sarah is staying here, and remember to leave your answerphone on in case I want to get in touch."

Okay ... So you'll have gathered by now that I'm an almost thirty-something, and I might be broken-hearted, but I'm definitely not looking for anyone else to whisk me down the aisle. Once was enough and I'm not going to spend my waking hours looking for a replacement. What we're talking about here is your everyday marriage, which nevertheless meant everything to me, going to the dogs because my husband, Will, found that he preferred the company (not to mention the bed) of another. It happens all the time – lavish wedding, exotic honeymoon, possibly just enough time for a kid or two (if you haven't had them before the wedding), and then the divorce. Only we hadn't got as far as the kids, just the kitchen units, and those will eventually be paid for by Will as part of the same guilt package which includes letting me have his share of the flat.

Juliet was still hovering uncertainly whilst I moved my bags into the hall, flapping her hands in the 'helpless female' way which has become second nature to her. Nobody would guess at the steely core which has seen off a second husband with an even larger divorce settlement than the first, profited from the substantial gifts of several wealthy admirers in recent years, and even now has a rich Conservative or two panting like overweight pugs at the end of her lead. All of which has led her to view my own predicament as a bit of an occupational hazard best overcome by finding a replacement as soon as possible.

"I'll phone you after the weekend," I promised as I ushered her through the front door. "And don't worry – Newquay isn't far away, and that's the 'new Riviera' – it will be heaving with surfers, so you never know …"

Chapter Two

W hy is it that no matter how hard you imagine yourself in a place or a situation, the reality is never what you thought? For instance, I'd selected the guest house because it hadn't imposed a supplement for a single room, but I hadn't quite been prepared for its distance from the sea. The blurb, which had included 'Sea view, B&B, *en-suite* to all rooms' would have been better as 'See view...', because whatever views the rooms had, they definitely didn't include the sea.

A narrow road, its tarmac disintegrating here and there at the sides, led steeply upwards from the Edwardian villa and was banked by grassy hummocks, which sheltered Tremorden Bay from sight even from the upper windows. I could smell the salt air, though, tantalising enough to fill me with a childish excitement and making me turn back from the window to tackle my luggage.

It was only just after midday; the early morning Western railways service had performed with an uncommon punctuality and there had been a taxi sitting outside the station. Now the rest of the day was before me.

When I'd unpacked my few belongings into the cavernous wardrobe which looked as if it had been installed when the house was built, I went swiftly downstairs in search of the sea, pushing away the unbidden thought that it would have been nice had Will been here to share it with me. Ridiculous thought anyway, because had we still been together we would have been spending our hard-saved money on a much more exotic location, of the type which Juliet would have definitely approved.

In the hallway, on a highly-polished half-table, was a selection of leaflets describing Walks and Excursions and Things To Do, but I ignored them. I certainly didn't need outings and coach trips and people being convivial in sun hats and white sandals. I would find my way about alone.

I couldn't avoid the enquiring figure of the propri-etress though, who wasn't going to be put off by my curt nod. Another mental picture shattered, because she was the antithesis of the stereotypical Cornish land-lady who had inhabited my imagination. Instead of the buxom farmer's wife with a round rosy face and sturdy outdoor arms, like in custard adverts, Gwen Jarrett had a long narrow face with a large amount of chin, giving her a horse-like expression that made you want to offer her a bag of hay. Her ironing-board figure was encased in a pristine white overall which suggested that the door on the left might be a dentist's clinic, had it not had a metal plate on it stating: *Residents' Lounge.*

She stepped in front of me, blocking the light from the open front door and lifting herself onto the balls of her feet; unnecessarily, as she was already a couple of inches taller than me. She swayed for a moment, but managed to maintain her equilibrium and smiled at me as she murmured, "Everything all right?"

"Yes, thank you," I replied, standing very still and staring at the glimpse of her dress in the 'V' of the overall – a blue silky number etched through busily with swirls of pastel colours like an impressionist's palette – so that the woman would move away.

But she stood her ground. "Off to do some explor-ing?"

"Hopefully."

"It's still a bit quiet here yet, for young people, being early in the season." Her voice was like Margaret

Thatcher's, carefully cultured to hide her origins but not quite succeeding.

"I wanted somewhere quiet."

Her pale eyes surveyed me speculatively, as if weighing up the possibilities as to why I should be here, alone. She stood to one side to let me pass, smiling in what could have been a benign way, but actually looking even more horse-like as the top of her dentures revealed themselves.

"We don't do evening meals of course, but you're welcome to some afternoon tea if you want to come back for a little rest later," she said. Perhaps she was marking me down as recuperating from a long illness and would try to swop anecdotes about her gallstones or somesuch, once I'd been here a few days.

"Thank you," I answered, holding my beach bag in front of me as I squeezed past so that I didn't brush against her rigid form. I could still feel her eyes on me as I went through the door, so it was good to step out into the fresh air. Trust me to choose a place that was probably Cornwall's answer to the Bates Motel! I had a brief flash of Will's face smiling indulgently at my aptitude for such errors, in the days when it was still an endearing quirk, not an irritation.

I didn't follow the steep little road, but strode out across the rough grass, the taller spikes pricking my bare legs, the light sea breeze sending only the smallest of puffball clouds scudding across the sky. The hummocks became sand dunes, occupied here and there by families sheltering from the breeze or an excess of sun, or from the enquiring eyes of other holidaymakers as they changed their clothes. I wound my way between them, the soft loose sand burning my feet as my sandals sank into it. I paused every now and again to scan the horizon and take deep appreciative breaths. This was what I remembered. Momentarily I was eight again.

The tide had gone out a long way and I took off my sandals to walk on the cool compact ridges it had left behind. It was too soon for the school holidays, so there were only a few families with very young children dotted about, building sandcastles and playing beach cricket with arbitrary rules and sponge balls, but I decided I wanted still more isolation. I walked purposefully across the curve of sand to the beginning of the headland where large rocks jutted out almost to the water's edge. Reaching them, I selected a large flat dark grey one, its front, where water had only recently sprayed it, as sleek and shiny as sealskin.

I made it my own. My towel was spread across it, my canvas shoulder-bag dropped by its side, my sandals neatly placed nearby, a paperback (selected impatiently with little real interest in its contents) laid on the towel – all these actions carried out with an economy of movement which I'd developed since I'd been on my own. Many times over the last few months I'd watched myself performing tasks with a precision which was totally alien to the person I'd once been.

Sitting on the rock, feeling its dry heat emanating through the towel, I hugged my knees and squinted out to sea, the midday sun too strong even for my very dark glasses. Everywhere was calm. Some sort of large funnelled boat moved slowly across the horizon, and the voices of the families on the beach, carried in the opposite direction by the breeze, were indistinguishable: faint, high-pitched hummings.

I exhaled very slowly. This is what I'd come for. Time to clear my mind, to think, to plan now that I was free.

Free? The word mocked me, a shallow substitute for *bereft, adrift,* a euphemism for *rejected.*

I hadn't thought it would be as bad as this. When I'd overcome the initial shock of Will's desertion, had absorbed his announced intention of setting up home with Lauren and had finally recognised the futility of clinging on to a marriage that was clearly dead, I'd expected to come to terms with it in as short a time as the split itself had taken.

There'd been well-meaning platitudes from friends

and family who thought they understood, but clearly didn't. The words of comfort eventually did nothing but grate on my already shredded nerves, and I'd had to force myself not to voice the hot retorts which remained trapped in my head instead.

"At least you're young enough to start again – it would have been much worse if you were ten years older." *Why? Because I would have a much harder time trying to find a replacement for the obviously defective model I was lumbered with last time? 'This one no good Madam? Well, don't worry, we'll have more in stock shortly.'*

"Thank goodness there are no children involved – it makes everything much simpler to cope with." *And after all, children would have perpetually reminded me that once upon a time I was wallowing in a happiness that must have been built on sand.*

And from my grandmother: "It could have been worse. You could have been widowed like I was and had your heart broken forever." *But why does a divorce imply that your fractured emotional state is only a temporary one?*

At times I wanted to shout that I wished Will *had* died. Because then he would have remained, in my mind and everyone else's, the person I'd been prepared to commit myself to for life, and the virtues I'd loved would have stayed intact and enshrined in the sanctity of the dead. Because then everyone would have accepted my lament for the happy times we'd shared; would have listened to my endless memories of our ecstatic early years; would have allowed me to have a past worth mentioning; would have accepted my grief as a genuine state and not a torrent of bitterness as they supposed and therefore tried to suppress. And would not have implied from what they said, and from what they omitted to say, that the marriage I'd entered into with all the optimism of one truly in love, and at the time loved in return, must have faltered through something lacking in me.

"You need taking out of yourself," declared Jodie, the only girl in the office younger than me, and she had insisted on taking me to wine bars and clubs and introducing me to her friends. But my barbed retorts to the less than inspired chat-up lines of men who had initially found my aloofness beguiling had been seen by Jodie and her friends as ingratitude, so that they had stopped asking me. And when I filled the interminable office hours with a new determination to keep my desk tidy, my filing up-to-date and my in-tray empty, Jodie had retreated even more puzzled, with suggestions that I seek counselling urgently.

But I'd already analysed my actions and didn't need anyone else to identify the reasons behind my altered behaviour. I found comfort in the repetitious tasks, rather like an abandoned child rocking backwards and forwards in its cot. I knew that by concentrating and completing every task in front of me I could push away the unwelcome reflections on what had happened, the hurt of rejection and the ugly pictures of my hopeless pleadings with him not to leave.

The tranquillity of the scene in front of me gradually ebbed the confused thoughts swirling round my head, and I knew that having allowed them their rein they would not intrude again at least for today. Now my head was filled with nothingness, a suspended state where I could think and feel little and which often, lately, came upon me at strange times so that making even the simplest decision, like what to have for supper, became impossible .

Suddenly, out of the corner of my eye, I became aware of a slight movement nearby, but resolutely refused to turn to it.

"It's all right," came a gravelly voice, "I'm not going to bother you. It's just that there are only two flattish rocks around here, and they're close together. And as you're sitting on the one I usually have, I'm going to use this one."

I turned then, ready with a hot retort, in case there was hidden animosity in the words. A tall, thin woman, in her late fifties I guessed, had flung her belongings onto the rock and was unbuttoning a pair of very faded shorts, revealing equally faded bikini bottoms. Her tan was as deeply ingrained in her skin as a fisherman's, so that she had to be a local who spent all summer outdoors. Light brown hair, bleached from the sun in places and showing signs of grey in others, which either had a natural wave in it or had not been brushed for several days, was pushed back from her face with a wide hairband, below which sapphire blue eyes surveyed me for a moment. Then, without any hint of self-consciousness, a T-shirt was pulled over her head to reveal a pair of bare breasts which sagged slightly as they settled back onto her chest, as brown and weathered as the rest of her.

"Don't worry," she flashed a grin at me, "that's as far as I go. No skinny-dipping – this is Cornwall, after all!"

The grin was infectious and I found myself smiling back. "Would you like your rock?" I asked.

But the woman was already spreadeagling herself on the other one. "No, this one's fine. I'll just have my daily dose of ultra-violet and all those other dreadfully harmful rays which do wonders for my poor joints and then I'll be gone." Her eyes were closed, but as I turned away she went on in a forthright way, "You'd better cover yourself with lashings of cream if you burn easily, though – the breeze hides the strength of the sun."

I lay back on my own rock, feeling ridiculously over-dressed in shorts and top, and returned to my thoughts. My intentions on coming away alone like this had been so varied, depending on the state of my emotions and my hormones, that now I'd arrived I couldn't decide just what I wanted. Solitude, where I could wallow in my grief but kid myself that I was 'recuperating', vied with the pragmatic side of my nature which told me that I should get down to making some concrete decisions about my future.

And despite what I had told Juliet, after months of enforced celibacy there *were* often sudden urges to have a wild fling with an impossibly handsome stranger who would find me irresistible, thus restoring my self-esteem while also exacting revenge on Will's treachery, even if I was the only one who knew about it.

My vacillations became lulled into a torpor by the soothing sounds of the sea and the heat of the sun. I had no idea how long I'd been drowsing when the woman's voice seeped into my consciousness again. "Time to go. The tide has turned, and it moves pretty quickly here. These rocks will be submerged soon."

She was already standing, pulling on her T-shirt, as I, still dragging myself away from the confusion of semi-sleep, sat bolt upright in befuddled alarm.

The woman laughed. "It's all right. You're not about to be engulfed immediately, I just thought I should warn you."

"Thank you," I said, easing myself off her rock and gathering my belongings in an unhurried fashion to show the woman that I was fully aware of the situation. I turned my back as I packed things in the canvas bag, expecting the woman to stroll away, but she stood watching me until I was ready to move off.

"Where are you staying?" She fell in beside me as we played stepping-stones back over the rocks, her long tanned legs and slim hips like those of a twenty-year-old. The wounded side of me hadn't intended to fall into conversation or strike up any sort of rapport with strangers to whom I might have to explain my present sorry state, but it was impossible not to reply.

"The Lansdowne."

The woman stood still and stared at me incredulously. "That dreadful place? On your own?" Then, before I could utter a word in defence of my choice, she went on: "Now you're going to tell me that Gwen Jarrett is a favourite aunt of yours and I will have put my big foot in it once more!"

But the wide grin back in place showed that she didn't really care if she'd offended anyone. Again, I found myself responding. "It sounded nice in the brochure."

"Oh, it undoubtedly is if you're over sixty, can't stand noise or kids and don't really like the seaside but come anyway because that's what you've done all your life."

"I thought I wanted peace and quiet when I booked it," I found myself divulging, in spite of myself.

The woman's eyes narrowed shrewdly as she glanced sideways at me. "And now you're here?"

It was my turn to stand still. "Now I'm not sure," I said.

"Well, at least it's only B&B, so you can get out and about all day. There's lots to do in the bay you know, and plenty of good places to eat and make friends – if that's what you decide you want." She thrust out her hand. "I'm Marsha, by the way. Everybody here knows me. Came here well over thirty years ago with a band of free-loving hippies, but they all eventually drifted back to London and became bank clerks or whatever, and I ..." She gave a short laugh. "Well, I just stayed. Come and search me out if you need a bit of company."

Her grip was strong and dry. If we'd met at a formal gathering, with her straightforward manner and rather eccentric easy confidence I would have put her down as an army officer's wife who in earlier times might have helped shape the sub-continent.

"I'm Allie," I replied. "Thank you; I may take you up on that."

Marsha nodded, and then purposefully moved off, striding along the beach at a quickened pace which indicated that she herself had no further need of my company for the present.

When she was quite some distance away, she turned and called, cupping her hands round her mouth so that I could hear. "A crowd of us will be at the Smugglers' tonight – join us if you like!" She didn't wait for me to call back, but simply waved and went on her way, and I found myself envying the easy ability to be friendly.

It had been a long time since I'd felt part of a crowd.

END OF SAMPLE CHAPTERS
"Just One More Summer" by Julie McGowan
can be purchased from all good online stores,
or better still, ask for it from your local independent
or chain book store.

About

JUST ONE MORE SUMMER

Devastated by the breakdown of her marriage, Allie flees to the one place her heart can seek comfort: Cornwall, where she hopes childhood memories of a holiday with her father will sustain her while she sorts out her plans for the future.

But fate has other ideas, and she finds herself drawn into an almost obsessive friendship with a band of strange bedfellows led by Marsha, an intense, ageing hippy with a powerful life force that at once comforts, stimulates and infuriates Allie.

Her growing attraction to one of the golden group's men, Adam, bewilders her as she discovers that nothing in life is what it seems, and the only constant is change. Little by little the layers of her past are painfully peeled away.

Initially ruffled and confused, and later deeply hurt by what she considers multiple levels of betrayal, Allie once again chooses flight. She heads back to London, but finds that her life-complications only deepen – her husband begs her to come back to him, her estranged father arrives unannounced from France, her loopy mother proclaims yet another marriage, Adam turns up to take her back to Cornwall – and the hardest part is yet to come for them all.

Finally, Allie realises that she must confront the secrets and lies of her past – and Marsha's – before she can face her own future.

DON'T PASS ME BY

Julie
McGowan

Don't Pass Me By: Sample Chapters

Chapter One

First, there was the blast. Then... silence. A complete and disturbing absence of any sound. No reassuring ticking of the clock that had kept Lydia company through many long evenings spent alone at the fireside. No creaking of floorboards. No whining of the cupboard door in the scullery as it swung back and forth on its hinges because it wouldn't close properly. Nothing.

As the first shock of the explosion began to recede, Lydia struggled to make sense of what had happened. She knew she had to move, although for the moment her brain felt too fuddled to work out why. There was just a need, an urgency that she couldn't identify. Tentatively she opened her eyes into the eerie quiet, forcing them to stay open against the grittiness of the brick dust that was swirling through the air as haphazardly as the confused thoughts swirling through her brain.

A huge orange halo lit the room from where the window, indeed the whole back wall, had been. It highlighted strange mounds of rubble and timber. Cold night air rushed in through the hole, aiding her return to consciousness. Into the silence came a thin, reedy, wail. Rescue workers, ambulances, perhaps.

She eased herself into a sitting position, wincing as her head made contact with the kitchen table. That must have been what saved her – she must have landed under the table as she fell. She winced again as she tried to push away some of the rubble around her feet. The wailing sound was increasing now, more insistent... more recognisable...

Grace! Grace was alive!

Suddenly Lydia was completely awake as the wailing turned into outraged howls. Her baby's need helped to push the pain away as she struggled to her feet, wincing this time from the sharp pain down her side.

She remembered now. It had nothing to do with the explosion.

"I'm coming!" she called, her voice croaky from the brick dust which had settled on the back of her throat. "I'm coming!"

As she began to clamber towards the front of the house, she found Billy lying immobile just a yard away from her, part of his body covered by fallen masonry. Perhaps he was dead.

The thought triggered no emotion. She forced her way into the hall.

The front part of the house seemed untouched apart from the layer of dust which had already penetrated everywhere. Grace was in her pram, unharmed, her limbs flailing in indignation that her demands were not being met with her mother's usual swiftness. *"Thank God,"* Lydia said of a deity she no longer believed in. *"Thank God."*

She lifted the crying infant into her arms, wiping her reddened distressed face with the edge of her cot sheet. "Sssh, ssh, you must be quiet while I think what to do."

She lowered herself onto the bottom part of the stair-case, the weight of the baby sending spasms of pain shooting from her side round to her back. The child's crying ended abruptly as she latched desperately onto the breast Lydia offered her, and while Grace sucked, Lydia tried to force her foggy brain to work.

It couldn't have been a bomb – there had been no air raid warning. She could only think of the gasworks in the next street. The surrounding houses would have taken the brunt of it, with the back of this house catching the tail end. Strange to think that they had all been waiting for the day when Hitler would send his bombs over and now their house – possibly their street – had been destroyed by what appeared to be an explosion at the gasworks.

The earlier part of the evening came back to her. Billy's anger. His army boots against her body as she writhed on the floor, crawling towards the shelter of the table for protection minutes before the blast. Ironically, it was that which must have saved her from further injury.

They must go, now, she knew, before the rescue workers arrived to deal not just with them, but with Billy also. But what if he was dead? Then there'd be no need for them to get away in a hurry. She had to check.

Soothed by her feed and tired from her prolonged bout of crying, the baby soon fell asleep. Lydia settled her in the pram and steeled herself to return to the back room, from where there had so far not been a sound.

Billy was lying in the same position. Very quietly Lydia moved towards him, stepping carefully so as not to dislodge the remnants of their home, lest she disturb him. There was a trickle of blood on his forehead, but otherwise his face was unharmed. Grey with dust, as was his hair, his relaxed features gave him an innocent, boyish look, belying her last sight of his face, contorted with fury. He looked as handsome as when they first met, when he had swept her off her feet.

She gave herself a mental shake. No time now for remembering. His left arm was lying free of the masonry which pinned his body to the floor. Gingerly she slid her hand around his wrist. There was a pulse. Faint, but steady.

At the same moment she thought she could hear voices shouting and she knew it wouldn't be long before helpers arrived, calling out for survivors, with torch-light playing around the desolation.

"Goodbye Billy," she whispered.

She made her way back past the sleeping baby and climbed the stairs. Her movements were deliberate, almost trance-like, as she forced herself to think only of the immediate need to get away with Grace. What had gone before and where their future lay could not, for the moment, be considered.

As below, the rear bedroom was devastated, but the bag she had already packed was sitting on the double bed at the front. She picked it up and tiptoed back down the stairs. Lifting the baby up and wrapping her in a shawl, she quietly stepped out through the front door into the night.

Chapter Two

T hey're coming! The car's just turned in at the gate!"
Rhian left her vantage point in the front porch
and flew into the kitchen, where her older sister
was buttering bread.

"How many?" Bronwen asked as she wiped her hands
on an old towel.

"I couldn't see. *Come on.*"

The two girls stood on the porch steps as the car
pulled up. In the front were their parents and in the
back sat a thin, dark-haired figure.

"It's a boy!" Rhian exclaimed. "Mam said we'd have
girls!"

Mam got out of the car. "Don't gawp, you two – he's
feeling shy enough already. I hope that kettle's not
boiling dry."

Bronwen scuttled back into the house, but Rhian
stayed to watch her Dad pull forward the passenger
seat and the young boy climb out. Her heart began to
beat more rapidly. *A boy! I wonder if he'll play with me.
Climb trees and make dams in the brook. And Dad will be
pleased to have a boy around.*

"Alright lad?" Dad was asking in his firm voice as the
boy straightened up and surveyed the girl as openly as
she was looking at him. He was several inches taller
than Rhian, wearing a crumpled school uniform with a
cap which sat askew as if not strong enough to subdue
the thatch of dark hair upon which it perched.

"This is my daughter Rhian, who's nine," Dad went on, "and the other girl, who's just gone inside is Bronwen, who's thirteen – so you see, you'll fit in very nicely with us."

Rhian said "Hallo" shyly, but he simply nodded slightly and looked about him as Dad lifted a battered cardboard suitcase and a gas mask out of the boot.

"Come on," he said, removing the cap and pressing it into the boy's hands. "You'll feel better when you get some of Mam's food inside you."

Rhian ran on ahead into the kitchen. Mam was talking to Bronwen as she bustled round the kitchen with her usual swift movements.

"Mr. Owain Owen had said he'd try and make sure we'd have a girl – it would just be easier with the two of you – but Mrs. Owain Owen said that was all that was left – the girls had all been accounted for. I don't know why *Mister* Owain Owen is the Billeting Officer – he doesn't get a word in when that wife of his is around..."

Rhian and Bronwen exchanged quick glances at this, because their own Dad rarely said a word when his wife was in full flow, but that was because she was chatty in a friendly way, not downright bossy like Mrs. Owain Owen. Aware of footsteps behind her, Rhian said loudly, "Dad told us to come through."

She moved further into the stone flagged kitchen and indicated the boy standing in the doorway. Mam's eyes swept over him. Rhian hoped he didn't see the pity in Mam's eyes as she surveyed his bedraggled state.

"Why don't you show Arthur where he is upstairs," she told Rhian, in the kind voice she used when her children were feeling poorly. "Bronwen, tell your Dad that he'd better come in for his supper now as well, before he starts seeing to the animals, because I won't be doing it twice."

The boy followed Rhian up the steep staircase, his feet clattering on the polished wooden steps.

"You'd better wash your hands, Mam always checks," she said, showing him the small bathroom. She coloured slightly. "The... er... lavatory's next door, if you need to go first."

But the boy washed his hands quickly under the cold tap, dried them skimpily on the towel Rhian proffered and then turned to her.

"I'm not stopping," he said.

"I think you have to," she replied. "Look, this is your room – you can see right across the farm from here."

She opened a door opposite the bathroom. Inside was a bed with a candlewick cover, a narrow wardrobe and a dressing table. The boy followed her in, looked through the window and then sat on the bed. Rhian felt hot all over again; would he be able to tell that there was a rubber sheet underneath the cotton one? Mam had been to a talk on evacuees at the Red Shed. "They all wet the bed, apparently," she'd said on her return.

"What's your name?" Rhian asked the boy now.

"Arfur," he said. "But I'm not stopping – not once me Mum's better, anyway."

"What's wrong with her?'

"She got hurt in the black-out. Broke her leg. There was no-one else for me to stay with, but I'm going back soon as she's better."

She wondered if she should say sorry about his Mam, but he didn't look as if he wanted her sympathy.

"You sound odd," was all she said instead. "Where are you from?"

"Bermondsey," he answered. "That's in London," he went on when he saw the blank look on her face. "But it's not me that talks funny, it's you lot."

He looked out of the window again.

"Where's all the other houses?"

"In the village – you'll have passed them in the car. We're at the end. Because we're a farm. Only a small one though. Cows in the flat fields and some sheep on the high ones. And we've got a pig."

He didn't seem to be listening to her chatter, but continued to stare out of the window.

"Will you climb trees with me?" Rhian asked after a

few moments.

He turned quickly back to her then.

"Girls don't climb trees!" he scoffed. "'Specially not little puny girls."

"Yes they do!" she cried hotly. "And I'm not puny! I'll show you!"

"No point," he said, "'cos I'm not gonna be stopping."

Bronwen was calling them from downstairs. But Rhian didn't hurry him out of the room. She surveyed him steadily instead, taking in his dark, hostile eyes, the hair that was now flopping over his forehead and the shabby pullover that looked too small for him.

Oh yes you are staying, she thought, with the same certainty that her Auntie Ginnie, once she had a small sherry and a Marie biscuit inside her, claimed to know things. One way or another, she knew he was going to stay in her life forever.

Chapter Three

The car bounced and bumped along the rutted road, but thankfully the baby still slept in Lydia's arms.

"It seems a bit of a long way in the car," the Billeting Officer's wife said from the front seat, as the road began to rise steeply on leaving the main street, "but it's easy by foot if you go through Amos's field – that's what the doctor usually does – on his bike most likely, whatever the weather – how he hasn't caught a chill I don't know…"

The woman talked on, whilst her husband concentrated on the lane which was taking them to goodness knows where. Lydia had little idea of where she was, except that it was hilly and remote, and at the moment she didn't care. She leaned her head on the back of the seat and hoped there would be time for a decent cup of tea before the baby woke demanding a feed. And perhaps something to eat – the sandwiches on the train seemed a long time ago.

It had been a long day. She had listened to the dawn chorus from a bench on the scruffy bit of waste ground which pretended to be a park some streets away from the night's devastation, before making her way to Sebastapol Street where the public baths thankfully opened early. The lady on the door had watched over the baby for an extra tuppence while Lydia bathed and changed into clean clothes. Then there had just been time for tea and a bun in a café before inveigling her way through the straggling lines of evacuees at the station and climbing unnoticed onto the train.

It had taken forever to reach Bridgend and then there'd been a wait for the change to a narrow branch line. Children were dropped off at various unpronounceable stops along the line, but Lydia had stayed put until they had reached this place and it was evident they were going no further.

The welcoming committee, consisting of a number of well-meaning ladies with sing-song voices, had put on quite a spread in the schoolroom, but the children had dived onto that, and Lydia had only managed a small piece of cake and a cup that was more milk than tea.

She was brought back to the present by the Billeting Officer, who rejoiced in the name of Owain Owen, clearing his throat preparatory to using a voice which probably didn't get much exercise when he was at home. He'd been efficient enough at the village school, though, dispatching the motley collection of children and the occasional mother to various houses and farms, ticking them off carefully on his clipboard. Until he came to Lydia, that is.

Then he'd resorted to checking through myriad forms and pieces of paper, muttering a few "I don't knows" before rifling through the papers again in the vain hope that they would, after all, throw up a solution for what to do with this young woman and her baby who were two bodies more than he'd been led to expect.

"I hope he's at home," he said now.

"He's at home," Mrs. Owain Owen said, with the satisfaction of one who knew the whereabouts of most of the locals at any given time. "Olwen Hughes saw him leaving the Matthews' house not half-an-hour since."

She swivelled her bulk around in the seat to address Lydia. "Terrible time Mrs. Matthews has been having with her old Dad – but the doctor's wonderful with him. Well, he's got a way with him – with almost everyone, the doctor has. Works ever so hard, he does – the only one here, now, see – even though he's got a dicky heart.

That's what's kept him here, instead of joining up, but we're not complaining. He'll be very pleased that I've found him someone so soon – bit of a shock it was when his last housekeeper up and left. None of us knew she'd been at all close to her sister, but when the call came that she was sick, well, off she went, just like that. But then they do say blood's thicker than water, don't they? Chapel, are you?"

Lydia started at this abrupt *non sequitur*. "Er... no... um... C of E – I was brought up C of E."

Now was probably not the time to tell the woman that she never wanted to see the inside of a church again.

Mrs. Owain Owen sniffed and turned back in her seat.

"Ebenezer Baptist chapel most of us go to round here – but there's one or two that go to St. Paul's." The last two words were uttered in a way that gave a clear indication of the low opinion she had of those few foolhardy souls. Her voice brightened again as they pulled up in front of a square, stone-built house.

"There you are, Owain," she nodded at the light shining from a front window. "Told you he was in. Quiet man, he is – keeps himself to himself," she told Lydia. "Except when he's with his patients, that is. Different man, then."

"No blackout," her husband said as he opened the car door. "He'll have to be told, doctor or no."

"It's nowhere near dark yet, man, there's no need to be such a stickler – 'specially out here – who's to see?"

Lydia eased herself and the baby out of the back seat as they continued to bicker. A cool wind whipped through her thin summer dress, making her instinctively hold the baby closer.

The light was just beginning to fade, and there was little sign up on this hillside of the hot sunny day through which they had travelled. She looked around at the raw beauty of the mountains which surrounded the village. There was a bleak majesty about their rounded tops rising above wooded areas here and there and fields which looked far too steep for man or beast to cope with.

Barely a sound could be heard apart from the shushing of the wind through the trees at the side of the house. She shivered slightly and followed the Owens up the steps to the front door, where Mrs. Owen had already tugged at a large bell pull.

It didn't take long for the door to be opened by a tall gaunt man with a towel in his hands.

"Ah! Doctor Eliot!" Mrs. Owen beamed at him and hoisted her Welsh accent up a notch or two. "Sorry to trouble you when you're probably getting your supper, but I think you'll be pleased when you know why we're here. Brought you a new housekeeper we have – extra evacuee from London she is, sort of surplus to requirements, you might say – so as soon as Mr. Owen here told me there was a bit of quandary, I thought of you – killing two birds you might say..."

She stepped back with a flourish, narrowly avoiding her husband's feet, and flung her arms wide to indicate Lydia, like a conjuror producing a rabbit out of a hat. Or, thought Lydia more darkly, like a procuress eager to please some eastern potentate.

The doctor, looking anything but pleased at the sudden offering brought before him, frowned as he peered out into the gathering gloom.

"A baby," he said. "You've brought a baby here?"

Mr. Owen cleared his throat. "I know it's a bit irregular, sir, you not being on the list for an evacuee" – he indicated the clipboard under his arm – "but we've run out of billets, sir, at least for the time being, and as my wife says, you're looking for a housekeeper, so..."

The doctor ran his hand through his hair, glanced down at the towel in his other hand, and said (still frowning, Lydia noticed), "Well, look, you'd better come in. We can't sort this out standing on the doorstep, but really, I don't think..."

He'd already turned and was leading the way into the house. Mr. Owen stood back before his wife and Lydia as they trooped into the room with the lights on: a rectangular space, save for the bay window at one end, with a small welcoming fire in the grate. It was furnished with several comfortable armchairs and a sofa, but no little nick-nacks or personal touches from a feminine hand. A masculine room, Lydia decided, plain and a bit austere – rather like its inhabitant, from first impressions.

The doctor stood before the fire and motioned them to sit down, but Lydia stayed on her feet, rocking the baby backwards and forwards.

"I've already advertised for a housekeeper," the doctor said, looking directly at the Owens.

"I know you have," Mrs. Owen replied, "but in all honesty, Doctor, you're not going to find another Miss Williams in a hurry. Those that haven't got their own families to see to are stepping into the breach left by the menfolk being away. And you must be finding it a bit hard on your own, what with the hours you have to keep…"

Her sharp button eyes surveyed the room, her fingers moving restlessly on her lap as if longing to wipe themselves across the layer of dust on the occasional table beside her to prove her point.

"Yes, but evacuees… children… I hadn't…" the doctor began, before Mr. Owen, slightly surprised at his own boldness, interrupted.

"Well, sir, I must tell you that if Miss Williams had still been here, I would have been obliged to place some evacuees with you, because of the space you've got. Not many houses of this size in the village, there aren't."

"The Joneses at Ton farm have taken four boys – all sharing one big bedroom," his wife added in impressed tones. "So a baby, with its mother to take care of it, shouldn't be any trouble."

It was at this moment, with the immaculate timing of the very young, that the baby decided to stir. Suddenly flinging out an arm, she gave a prolonged and lusty wail, her face reddening with the effort.

Unperturbed, Lydia sat herself on the sofa and unbuttoned her dress, turning away slightly until the baby was suckling. A strand of wavy brown hair fell across her face as she crooned gently to her child.

"Oh!" Mrs Owen said, shock at the brazenness of feeding one's child in front of others – in front of *men* – leaving her momentarily speechless, while her husband passed the rim of his hat through his hands, round and round, his gaze fixed intently on the fireplace.

"I'll draw your curtains, sir," he said, jumping to his feet at this solution to his embarrassment. "The blackout, you know – it must be lighting up time by now."

He moved swiftly round behind the sofa at the doctor's nod, easing the heavy curtains along their pole with consummate care and deliberation.

"Perhaps you'd like another room, my dear – the kitchen maybe?" Mrs. Owen asked, a hint of steeliness in her voice.

Lydia lifted her head, brushing the strand of hair away.

"No. Thank you. This is fine." She would have liked to ask for a glass of water because feeding the baby always produced a raging thirst, but she was aware of the need to impress upon this man that she was not going to be any trouble.

The doctor, apparently oblivious to the embarrassment felt by the other two, directed his gaze sharply towards her when he heard the low soft tones of her voice.

"Where are you from?" he asked.

"Bermondsey," she replied, her eyes back on the baby. "Our house was damaged by a gasworks explosion."

He frowned, his rather heavy dark eyebrows almost meeting. News of the explosion had been on the morning wireless. But he was surprised that she had been caught up in it. He'd met plenty of people from the East End when he'd been working in London, and this self-possessed young woman didn't sound like any of them.

"And your husband?"

"He's... he's dead... killed... abroad."

There was a moment's silence.

"I'm sorry," the doctor said, while Mrs. Owen tutted

softly and looked sorrowful. "But do you have no other family? Isn't there someone you could have gone to?"

"There's no-one," she said, dropping her head again to look at the baby.

"Well, Doctor Eliot?" Mrs Owen asked. It was all very well showing respect for the dead, and she was very sorry that this child was going to grow up without a father, but she was also aware that her husband couldn't fiddle with the curtains any longer but had no intention of moving back into the middle of the room. "What are we going to do?"

"There isn't much *I* can do, is there, Mrs. Owen?" he replied, his tone conveying to Lydia at least that he had been placed in an impossible situation. "Mrs.... I'm sorry, I don't know your name?"

"Dawson," Lydia said. "I'm Lydia Dawson."

"Mrs. Dawson had better stay here for now – a trial period, perhaps, and we'll see after that."

"Thank you, Doctor." Mr. Owen skirted round the edge of the room and held his hand out. "I knew you'd be able to help out. Very grateful we are, very grateful. And I'm sure you won't be disappointed," he added, as if he'd just supplied the man with a new household appliance.

The two men moved into the hall. Before she followed them, Mrs. Owen leaned over Lydia, torn between sympathy for this young woman and a desire to do things properly.

"We usually show a bit more discretion – a bit of decorum, in these parts, you know – when there's a baby to feed," she whispered, the feather sticking out of the brim of her brown felt hat nodding in time with her head.

She moved back slightly at the challenging look she received from the girl's deep brown eyes. "I've shown more bosom than this in an evening gown," she said, "and all the men were happy to look then."

Mrs. Owain Owen pursed her lips until they were etched in small vertical lines. For one of the few times in her life she wondered if she'd made a mistake. Perhaps this young woman, whom she'd realised from the start was different from the rest of the recent arrivals, was more of a hussy than she'd thought. Evening gown indeed! In Bermondsey?

"I'll be along with my husband in a few days to see how you're settling in," she said now, her tone haughty and formal.

"Thank you," Lydia said simply. "I'm sure we'll be fine."

Mrs. Owen opened her mouth as if to say more, but the baby suddenly lifted her head and turned towards the woman, fixing her with intense blue eyes and bestowing upon her a wide milky smile.

"Oh! There now. There now," she said, her own features softening in response. "Isn't she a little beauty! "She stared at the baby for a few moments before abruptly turning way. "I must go. Mr. Owen will be wanting his supper."

"Well done," Lydia said to the baby, dropping a kiss on her silky head as the door closed. She was rewarded with a resounding burp.

She could hear more talking in the hall as she settled the baby on her other breast and it was several minutes before the door opened again. This time the doctor came in alone, bringing with him her large battered hold-all.

"Is this all your luggage?"

She nodded. "I got told off because it was bigger and heavier than we were supposed to bring, but I explained that all the baby's things were in it as well."

His frown, which seemed to be habitual, deepened. "No, I meant is this *all* your luggage? What about all the bits and pieces you need for the baby – I don't have anything here... cots and so on..."

Lydia transferred the baby to her shoulder, deftly buttoning her dress with her free hand, stifling a smile. He'd obviously never visited the East End and seen how few cots were about, even before the war began.

"Do you have a chest of drawers in your spare room?" she asked.

"Of course."

"And a bucket in the kitchen?"

"I should imagine so – Miss Williams was always mopping and cleaning."

"Then that's all the bits and pieces I need for Grace. Perhaps you could show me – the room?" she went on as he continued to look sceptical.

"Oh yes... yes of course... it's this way."

He picked up the hold-all again and led her up the steep staircase whose dark stained wooden banisters added to the feeling of gloom pervading the hallway as daylight began to fade.

"This is Miss Williams' old room," he said, opening a door to the left of the landing. "My room's on the other side, and there are two smaller rooms at the back – perhaps one would do for the baby... I don't know... and there's a bathroom at the back too – with a bit of a temperamental geyser for the hot water, I'm afraid..."

He stood aside to let her enter. After the tenebrous hall, she gave an involuntary gasp of pleasure as she stood inside the door.

Immediately to her right was a wide, deep window with, through the lace curtains covering its lower half, the same view she had seen from outside. But from this height one could see all the way down the valley, with the very last of the evening sun glinting here and there on the river which wound its way between the rounded hillsides.

"Interlocking spurs," she said.

"I'm sorry?"

She turned to the doctor with a smile. "Interlocking spurs – the way the hillsides fit into one another – it's about the only thing I remember from school geography lessons!"

She surveyed the rest of the room. In front of the window was a small marble topped table with, next to it, a mahogany rocking chair. She had a fleeting mental picture of herself nursing the baby in this chair, a gentle breeze lifting the lace curtain through the open window.

She gave herself a mental shake. *You're here to work as the housekeeper. There won't be much time for sitting in rocking chairs.*

END OF SAMPLE CHAPTERS
"Don't Pass Me By" by Julie McGowan
can be purchased from all good online stores,
or better still, ask for it from your local independent
or chain book store.

About

DON'T PASS ME BY

1940: London is about to be ravaged by the Blitz. For Lydia the last beating is the final straw. She has to escape from her husband, and when a gas explosion rips their house apart she flees, taking baby Grace with her. Rejected by her father, and not knowing where to go next, she joins a crowd of evacuee children at the railway station, and her destiny is changed forever as they find themselves in rural Wales.

Don't Pass Me By is the story not only of Lydia and Grace's salvation, but of the lives of a handful of evacuee children transplanted from the city to a tiny village filled with strangers who speak a different language. Torn away from their parents, each child learns to cope – one with a farm full of fearsome animals and a warm, caring family; others not so lucky. From the love and compassion of many, to sinister abuse from a few, the children find different ways to survive their own catastrophes, while Lydia finds what she has always been seeking – but when her masquerade of widowhood is shattered, will she lose everything?

Don't Pass Me By is author Julie McGowan's third book, and the second based in her much-loved homeland of Wales. Her first, The Mountains Between, became a regional best-seller. Her second book, Just One More Summer, is a wonderfully intricate read based in Cornwall.

ROSE & CROWN, BLUE JEANS, BOATHOOKS, SUNBERRY, CHRISTLIGHT, and EPTA Books

MORE BOOKS FROM SUNPENNY BOOKS
www.sunpenny.com

A Little Book of Pleasures, by William Wood
Blackbirds Baked in a Pie, by Eugene Barter
Dance of Eagles, by JS Holloway
Don't Pass Me By, by Julie McGowan
Fish Soup, by Michelle Heatley
Just One More Summer, by Julie McGowan
Moving On, by Jenny Piper
Someday, Maybe, by Jenny Piper
Sudoku for Christmas (full colour illustrated gift book)
The Long Way Home, by Janet Purcell
The Mountains Between, by Julie McGowan

FROM BOATHOOKS BOOKS

A Whisper on the Mediterranean, by Tonia Parronchi
Far Out, by Corinna Weyreter
Watery Ways, by Valerie Poore

FROM SUNBERRY CHILDREN'S AND YOUNG ADULTS

If Horses Were Wishes, by Elizabeth Sellers
Sophie's Quest, by Sonja Anderson
The Lost Crown of Apollo, by Suzanne Cordatos
The Skipper's Child, by Valerie Poore
Trouble Rides a Fast Horse, by Elizabeth Sellers